Dare to Love in Oz

William Maltese

Savant Books
Honolulu, HI, USA
2009

Published in the USA by Savant Books and Publications
2630 Kapiolani Blvd #1601
Honolulu, HI 96826
http://www.savantbooksandpublications.com

Printed in the USA

Edited by Daniel S. Janik
Cover design by Deana C. Jamroz

ISBN: 0-9841175-4-7
EAN-13: 978-0-9841175-4-3

Dedication and Acknowledgement

For Laura Baumbach and Deana Jamroz, without whom this book's marvelous cover graphic wouldn't have been possible, and for Daniel S. Janik, editor and publisher extraordinaire, without whom this book wouldn't be able to call Savant Books and Publications its "home."

Table of Contents

Dare to Love in Oz

One

"Kenk-lum-ra!" Gerald Simms pointed. His low voice promised the worst was over; his optimistic smile, that crinkled the edges of his velvety black eyes and deepened his already deep dimple, bolstered that promise.

Kenk-lum-ra was an actor-player in aborigine Dream Time. To Jane Mylor, disinclined to believe in mythical battles waged by half-men-half-monsters against half-men-half-animals, *Kenk-lum-ra* was only a long-standing, very dead tree. If pressured, Jane might have conceded it simply a misnomer in an otherwise flat landscape without another tree, dead or alive, visible for miles. That the desiccated gum tree, bleached skeletal white by the never-kind elements of the Australian outback, hadn't been carted away, piecemeal, to fuel a fire in a locale where firewood was rarer than gold, was supposedly proof-positive of its Dream-Time origins. Jane, on the other hand, suspected the tree's stick-figure existence, supported atop bone-dry earth by a root system as dead as the deadweight it supported, was more a case of no one, in his right mind, wanting to stop in such an inhospitable spot to roast marshmallows, or to camp-fire broil wieners.

"Home base should be close enough to walk," Gerald offered; the Australian-blown dust had frosted his black hair with dull reddish highlights.

Jane wasn't encouraged. *Kenk-lum-ra*, although sighted clearly from their car, was still a good ways distance. The Facility, their ultimate destination, was even farther afield. Such miles might be walked easily on a good day, in ideal conditions, in an American suburb, but in a storm, in the wilderness area of Australia's

Northern Territory? "What's the bit about counting one's chickens before they're hatched?" She ran her fingers through her own dust-dulled black hair as more whirlwinds whipped up outside and obliterated all signs of the just-sighted landmark.

A mile later, Jane's hazel eyes squinted to rediscover the whereabouts of *Kenk-lum-ra* from within the rapidly thickening, stormy miasma swirling about them, when a blinding flash of lightning impressively materialized, its upper limits lost amid the multi-layered dust-blankets ripped apart to let it through, its leading-edge spearheading into the ground. There was an accompanying ear-splitting and earth-shaking boom of loud thunder.

In the immediate aftermath, while Jane struggled to erase from her retinas the retained negative image of the bolt, a skeletal arm of *Kenk-lum-ra* rammed through and shattered car windscreen, threatening to impale her, like a vampiress on a wooden stake.

"Jane!" Gerald's worry was palpable underneath

the howling wind that had rejoined them along with the serrated tree limb thrust inside the stopped and violated car. "You all right?"

Jane thought not. The incongruousness of her feeling suddenly so wet in a place so dry emphasized that things were not the way they should be.

"Right, that'd be the water bag ruptured," Gerald diagnosed her misinterpreted symptoms. "That's two up, and we've just begun."

The sun-and-wind-bleached limb had driven through the glass, and barely missed Jane and Gerald, stabbing the canvas and draining most of their precious water reserve. The branch continued on into the seat between them.

But the damage hadn't stopped there. *Kenk-lum-ra*'s bulk had dropped atop the vehicle's hood and roof, severely compacting the car's interior; the tree trunk and several branches blazed lightning-lit, adding inky, caustic smoke to the already storm-polluted air.

"What about you?" Jane's voiced concern was

late in coming, but not because her concern hadn't been there all along. She was encouraged that Gerald looked okay across the wooden barrier thrust between them like a disapproving duenna.

"A scratch here, a scratch there," he assessed his personal damage.

"I'm not sure my door will open." Jane was spurred to that admission by a shift of wind that fanned outside flames dangerously in her direction. She didn't relish dying on a pyre fueled by wood as rare as the precious water that continued soaking her.

Her door was squeezed flat by the raw tonnage of the fallen tree. Thankful for years of yoga stretching exercises that kept her supple, if never as thin as she'd like, she braced against branch and door. One foot pressed down on the door handle; both feet pushed outward; the barrier screamed in protest.

Jane was shocked by the unexpected suddenness of her success: the complete door dropped out with a thud that summoned a geyser of dry ground from the dust-pile below that caught and cushioned it.

"*I* should be so lucky!" Gerald congratulated.

"Need help?" Flushed with success, she could be magnanimous.

"I believe if I suck in my gut and contort like a pretzel, I might manage to squeeze out over here. In the meantime, I'll attempt to save what I can of our water supply, if you'll scrounge for anything else we might need when we're out of here."

Kenk-lum-ra's flames remained unruffled by the oppressive atmosphere that would have squelched any less persistent conflagration. The fire fed additional heat to a day already warmed to excess by the greenhouse effect caused by an invisible sun above them oven-baking the storm. As scientists, Jane and Gerald knew where that sun should be, put there by scientific laws and mathematical principles, but they couldn't make out even a hint of its ghostly circle from within thick haze.

A gunnysack, brought for stuffing under the car wheels in case the vehicle got stuck and needed the additional traction, became their carryall into which Jane stuffed all the candy bars she could rob from the crushed glove compartment that surrendered its cache of goodies only under protest. She added a very-dented-but-still-operative flashlight and some first-aid supplies.

Gerald's contribution was less visibly impressive, but looks deceived, because the water bag, skillfully sutured to less than a fourth its original size and contents, would be of key importance over a distance that, although not all that far as the crow flies, was plenty far to drop both Gerald and Jane from dehydration.

The two-way radio was worthless; its cracked and fractured console said it all. It hadn't worked in the storm anyway.

"Kilbooling Cave, then?" Gerald suggested. The cave was made to order. Long-since abandoned, it had once been a gathering place for the nomadic aborigines by whom *Kenk-lum-ra* was originally named. The cave had been carved by the elements from a hard face of pink sandstone that had survived where less sturdily cemented

7

features had long since dissolved into tiny, individual granules of swirling, biting sand. If the cave was on a less-than-direct route to The Facility, it offered at the least a place to rest before moving on.

"Kilbooling Cave it is," Jane agreed, voicing her reasons why: "The car, in its present state, offers little protection; the fire, fading, and then flaring, could fan to dangerous proportions at any time; our water supply won't last very long if we stay exposed as we are in this heat; and The Facility isn't really all that far away."

Gerald commandeered the compass from the dashboard, Jane the smaller compass from the survival gear. Disorientation in such a situation had to be prevented, if at all possible.

"To further lessen the chances of my losing you," Gerald stated with finality, offering Jane the end of a rope to loop about her waist while tying the other end about his.

"You mean to lessen *my* chances of losing *you*!?" She smiled good-naturedly, paying for the gesture by swallowing sand in her effort.

They took separate compass readings that—
thank God—concurred.

In the end, it proved difficult going. Walking the
storm was rat-on-a-treadmill difficult: it took all of their
effort to get almost nowhere.

It was impossible to see, and soon both
developed an automatic tendency to walk with eyes shut.
Where their skin wasn't red-raw, it was sandblasted,
vibrating painfully at the slightest touch of their dirt-
stiffened clothing.

Within minutes, the advantages of being
fastened together became obvious as poor visibility left
Jane relying upon the tension on the rope to assure her
that Gerald was still up ahead. Whenever the relied-upon
tension suddenly went slack, it seemed heart-stoppingly
probable to Jane that she'd lost him. Gratefully, this time
before total panic set in, she stumbled into him where
he'd stopped.

"What?" she asked in response to some guttural,

wind-stolen words he had muttered.

Gerald repeated himself, but it was the accompanying extension of his arm that more clearly conveyed his message. A sandstone outcropping had appeared momentarily and then disappeared, dissolving back into the churning dust.

"Do you remember what the cave opening looks like?" Gerald shaded his eyes with a hand as if he feared sunstroke from the still invisible sun.

Jane heard him, but only barely. "It's that way, I think!" She pointed north along a barely visible wall of pink stone whittled into grotesque folds by the wind shear.

The entrance, once they found it, wasn't large. They had to pass through one at a time; each stooping in the process, bowing submissively as if begging permission to enter. Almost immediately, though, it widened and angled comfortably higher and wider into sheer rock. The floor ascended on a steep incline rendered by myriads of bygone feet into a gentle, natural stepladder.

Jane fished for the flashlight in the gunnysack.

"Tell me, do I have any skin left?" Gerald asked, rubbing a caked combination of sweat and dust from his dark eyes. A sweep of his arm offered Jane the first go at the crude stairway.

Jane hesitated. "I've never liked this place, even before I lost a tiger snake in here, three months ago, on a sample-gathering excursion."

"That's a none-too-cheery incentive to hurry along. However, I doubt that snake has stuck around to bid you a friendly hello and thanks. Do you?"

"I tried to snare it outside, but it was inside here in nothing flat." Jane didn't like snakes; no matter that she'd spent a lifetime of concentrated effort to confine her fear of them so she could work with the reptiles when her work called for it. Her dislike, never far beneath the surface, made her more cautious than she might have been and had saved her from more than one snake bite that might have resulted from carelessness born of confidence.

"Want me to go first?" Gerald: a knight in shining armor.

"Nah! As you said: it's hardly likely to be hanging around after I scared the daylights out of it with that noose on the end of the pole."

The climb emptied them into a large interlocking "room"; this one was lit via a series of faults in the roof and walls, the sickly light forming ghostly images of dust-clogged columns, tubes, and sheets in the air. The same openings reluctantly admitted gusts of wind transformed by the passages into low, gooseflesh-raising moans. Petroglyphs, white, red, brown, pink, and ocher, created in another time by aborigine artists mixing water and spit with pulverized rock, competed for attention among depictions of men and animals, many with visible internal, as well as external organs. Representations of kangaroos, wallabies, koalas, wombats, dingoes, emus and kookaburras seemed to dance between totems of half-human-half-animal beings and older single-line drawings supposedly done not by men but by spirits, *Mini*, who melted into the cliff walls, leaving only soul-like shadow-marks in passing.

"Tribal leaders once instructed aborigine young men here." Gerald, too, was caught up in the strange, otherworldliness of this place that he imagined once housed pagan religious rituals for rites of passage. "Can you visualize the corroboree: dancers gyrating in portrayal of aborigine Dream Time, their bodies as intricately and colorfully decorated as these on the walls, rhythmically clapping hands and thumping the ends of hollow-stick didgeridoos on the floor?"

Jane hesitated. "I see Dracula's mausoleum complete with dust-dance and wind-song dirge. Frankly, this place gives me—always has—the proverbial creeps."

"So, let's eat and run."

"Agreed."

Neither voiced the other more compelling reason for a short stay: sandstorms were known to blow with increasing strength, nonstop, for literally days on end.

Gerald and Jane detached, and Gerald squatted, drawing abstracts of the outside world, like the ancients had done before him, onto the dust-covered hard, compact earth of the floor. Jane dropped down beside him.

"Here *we* are." A knife materialized, seemingly from the air, its point tracing an x-marks-the-spot. "Over this way, there's The Facility." His knife point shifted. "I figure we've only two alternatives for shelter en route."

"Minor outcroppings here," Jane pointed with a finger; she was as familiar with the area as he was. "Or here."

"Your vote?"

"This one." Her finger shifted back to the first. "It offers more potential. No caves but deeply weathered indentations all around; no matter the wind direction, there'll be a place to catch our breath. The other is too wedge-shaped; a stiff wind from the wrong direction could leave us exposed on two sides."

"I concur."

"We do rather agree on an awfully lot, don't we?" she offered, amending, "So far."

"What we have is obviously a team made in heaven."

"What we have is a team made by extenuating circumstances," Jane added cautiously.

"Spoilsport!" he chided, pursing his lips in what he meant to pass for a pout. "For that, I get dubs on the 'Coconut-Almond' candy bar."

"So our team-made-in-heaven is about to end up in an out-and-out brawl over a dipped-in-dark-chocolate bar?" In fact, Jane wanted the "Peanuts and Caramel" bar she had carefully nestled at the bottom of the canvas bag, but the playful repartee provided a much appreciated respite in a situation otherwise devoid of enjoyment.

"To preserve peace, I'll take the 'Peanuts and Caramel'," he said.

Jane laughed; she couldn't help it. They were obviously on the same wavelength.

Gerald felt Jane's certain "something." "What makes me think the 'Coconut-Almond' was never really a bone of contention, while the 'Peanuts and Caramel' bar, on the other hand ..."

"Actually, I'd trade my whole allotment of candy for one good drink of water."

"No need to barter. The drink is on the house." He extended the surgically repaired container; the accompanying slosh of water was as inviting as it was pitiful.

"Maybe I'll hold off a bit longer." She pushed the bag back towards him with the back of a hand, but Gerald wouldn't accept.

"Let me tell you a little story," he said, offering her the bag once again.

"Please, not another of your Dream Time stories."

"This about a guy I know who was out for fossils in the Gobi."

"Already I get the connections: desert, thirst.

Right?"

"And: separation from modern conveniences. And: only half a canteen of water."

"Sounds downright Aesopic."

"Come on now, give me a break! You're going to like this one." Gerald ran large, well-shaped fingers through his dusty hair, rearranging some of the more disrupted strands back into a semblance of order.

"Okay, about this guy . . ." she conceded.

"Name was Tarrington. Zanner Tarrington."

"Zanner Tarrington, in the Gobi, cut off from all amenities, with only half a canteen of water," she summarized for him.

Gerald settled against the wall, the water bag tight against his chest, his arms folded across his knees; despite all the petroglyphs, none of them, as far as Jane was concerned, was as superb a piece of artwork as the man in front of her. She decided it was probably the dim lighting further fogging her brain battered by the baking heat, swirling dust, and by the severe wind-howl. Then again, it was, also, possible that it was just, plain and simple, that Gerald was an exceptionally handsome man.

"Zanner walked and walked. Each time he stopped, he contemplated his water. He told himself it was precious, and he'd die soon after he finished what little was left. When he was finally rescued, dehydrated, out of his mind and ready for death, he still had half a canteen of water. He'd have been far better off to have drunk it."

"Surely the inherent logic of your story is flawed somewhere. However ..." She accepted the again proffered water bag, unfastened the drawstring Gerald had improvised to keep the contents secured, and tipped the bag just enough to run a bit of water off the lip of one canvas fold and into her mouth. She didn't spill a precious drop.

"You've survived such conditions before?" Gerald was impressed; less by her drinking skill, which he expected, than by the fine line of her neck as her head tilted back for the water. There was something about the sheer purity of the gentle curve from her chin to the delicate notch at the base of her throat that struck him as marvelously beautiful, poetically sensuous, and more than just a little sexy.

"Well, there was that time in Baja, California." Who was she kidding? That time with Henry Pix was definitely not like the present with Gerald Simms.

Gerald took a final swig of water while Jane broke out the selection of candy; both left the "Peanuts and Caramel" for the other amid mutual aren't-I-the-selfless-one smiles. That bar went uneaten.

"Shall we take a look up top, then, before we pull out?" Gerald folded his wrapper and placed it in his pocket. Littering was something of which he heartily disapproved, even in an as out-of-the-way spot as this one. He still got upset about the time in the wondrously pristine Negev Desert, alone, watching a big-pronged ibex eating grass, when a rusted tin can blew in out of nowhere and spoiled the moment.

"Well, I suppose, since we're here . . ." Jane

would have preferred getting on their way. So far, the stopover hadn't been half-bad, though there had always been something about this place that left her decidedly uneasy, even more decidedly now. On the other hand, it was possible that her paranoia was more the result of being caught in a sand-blaster storm, attacked by a killer tree, and left abandoned with a passel of unpleasant memories than it had to do with the cave. Maybe.

Unconsciously copying Gerald, she slipped her candy wrapper into a pocket and came to her feet, promising her exhausted mind twenty-four-hours of uninterrupted sleep once she got back to the comparative comforts of her quarters at The Facility. Not to be outdone, she then promised her dust-caked body a very long, very hot shower.

They crept upwards hugging close to the wall, glimpses of Dream Time monsters flashing out of the corners of their eyes. Jane tried to concentrate on Gerald; he was definitely pleasing to look at. She'd always known he was handsome, but analyzing the "how" was proving difficult. It had something to do with the slight, almost Tartar slant of his high cheekbones, the square of his jaw, the straight line from the center of his forehead to the tip of his nose, the gentle concave of an always almost-but-not-quite-laughing dimple in the cleft of his chin.

He had a small birthmark hidden in the hairline of his right temple. Jane couldn't say how that birthmark included itself in his total package of attractiveness. Nor was she as yet willing to admit as to finding his lips, taken alone, too full and sensuous.

"What you see is what you get—if you're nice and say, *Please*." He'd caught her in her staring. His smile put his too-full lips to good advantage over his too-large, too-even, too-white teeth.

Jane was glad when they'd reached the access to the "roof." It gave her the opportunity to veer the conversation. "You want to go first, or shall I?" she asked.

"You got your 'firsties' when we came in," he

reminded and stepped by her into the crawlspace that slanted upward toward a distant hole made fuzzy by the churning dust outside.

"If you run into that tiger snake that escaped my specimen bag, give it my best." Jane liked the low, rumbling timbre of his responsive laugh as she commenced following him on hands-and-knees.

Halfway up, the wind began roaring; an irritant that accompanied her all of the way to the top.

A strong hand appeared from out of the dust cloud and grabbed hers, assisting her out of the hole. Good thing, too, because a gust unbalanced her. It was Gerald's handhold alone that kept her from losing her footing.

Though there was plenty of surface area on top of the roof, little of it was flat enough to use for standing, and its irregularity gave Gerald the excuse he needed to wrap his arm about Jane's waist, offering them both better anchorages against the suddenly increasing fury of the wind. Jane was surprised to find herself deriving a good deal of reassurance from his nearness. She was, however, less enthusiastic about the view, or, rather, lack thereof. They might be airborne within a cloud of dust for all she could see.

She knew where The Facility should be, just as she knew where the sun should be and where the sky should be. "I don't see a thing!" she told the wind, certain Gerald couldn't hear her—if not for the resonance of her words in her head, she would have doubted she'd even said them.

She was ready to beat a hasty retreat but yielded to Gerald's grip about her and his unvoiced invitation to stay a bit longer. They were rewarded with a momentary parting of dusty waves.

"Moses couldn't have done better," Gerald said; Jane actually heard him and smiled.

Through the powdery gloom, The Facility materialized like a futuristic settlement on a desolate Martian landscape. Its geodesic dome and its twelve acres of glass-gabled solar piping, the latter for distilling the brackish water bored from deep in the desert's depths, was beatific, as if suddenly revealed by God, while simultaneously instilling a sense of oddly cold and surreal salvation.

Between The Facility and where they stood, two lights suddenly appeared and moved towards them in unison.

"Car lights!" Gerald pointed as the vision was swallowed back into the body of the dust cloud.

Gerald and Jane slid back down into the cave, feet-first.

"A rescue team?" Jane shuddered at the sight of a half-man-half-snake inscribed in bloody red and macabre black aborigine-paint on the rose-tinted wall directly behind Gerald and staring menacingly over his shoulder at her.

He saw her shiver and reflexively offered her the warmth of his arm and body; she took both in the spirit in which they were intended; they nullified much but not quite all of the ominous chill griping her.

"They'd have to be crazy to send anyone out in a storm like this," he argued. "Even if they knew we needed rescuing, which is doubtful. They would most probably have assumed that I had sense enough to detour to Keerborg to sit out the storm."

Mention of Keerborg didn't bolster Jane's own confidence in her own common sense. Intuition had totally deserted her when, at Keerborg, she had paused en route to The Facility, after holiday in Sydney, when she had gotten word that Gerald had just made a mercy run of snake scrum to Sylan Springs. It was her chance to intercept him at Denbook Gulch—for a combined beat-the-storm race back to the lab.

Actually, Jane's anxiousness to leave Keerborg was, she knew, spawned by reasons much more complex than a desire to return quicker to her job.

For one, she'd been out to delay another of those always-to-be-dreaded blind dates well-meaning people were forever setting up for her. This one was with a Cole Wilcott, having been arranged by Mrs. Cooper, the owner of the bed-and-breakfast where Jane had spent most of her vacation. Well-known-throughout-Australia but painfully-photo-shy Cole had been contracted to meet Jane at Keerborg and fly her to The Facility. He had, however, radioed her from Grenpewrie Station that he had been forced down there by a storm-in-progress.

For two, an aborigine named Shem who had an uncanny "knack for prophesy" well-known in Keerborg had predicted "one helluva catastrophic blow" the likes of which undoubtedly would have kept Jane from The Facility for days if she didn't run for it while she had the chance.

Shem's intuitiveness, however, wasn't nearly as celebrated as that of his absent-from-Keerborg-on-a-quest father, Noah. Noah's predictions were right one-hundred percent of the time. Shem and Noah, neither of whom could possibly be mistaken by locals as prophets in the Christian sense, had been gifted their names by local missionaries who had found the aboriginal dialect unpronounceable. Jane suspected it was also an attempt to deflect the local folk from questioning what was a flagrantly pagan gift.

For three, Jane had been anxious to leave Keerborg, because she felt she had likely overstayed the welcome originally extended by Riala Murphy. Riala, as much as she denied it, still blamed The Facility, and, by association, those scientists in residence (Jane included?), for the death of Riala's brother. In time, of course, Riala would eventually come around to the obvious conclusion that the blame for her brother's death lay solidly on Leith Murphy, himself, who had no business out in hundred-plus-degree heat, chasing a snake all over the side of a rocky slope given Leith's congenital heart condition. The rest of the blame would probably always rest with Dr. Ralph Powers, the only person at The Facility besides Leith, who knew of the young man's health problem. Powers had been Leith's colleague in the mad attempt to catch the snake. Both men had apparently forgotten all potential for disaster in the excitement of trying to be the first to get hold of a reptile never before seen before by the entire scientific community. It hadn't helped matters that Leith had ended up getting bitten by the specimen, initially wrongfully casting the blame on the reptile given that the snake's venom was after the fact determined by Ralph to be non-toxic.

"A penny for your thoughts," Gerald interrupted Jane's reverie, spiriting her back to reality.

"It was a car!" Jane stated firmly. The desert was in the best of times a veritable "funhouse" of optical illusions. Hadn't she once seen a blue lake where there was nothing but desolate salt flats; hadn't she on another occasion seen horses grazing lush pasture where there'd been only endless sand?

"I agree!" Was this wishful thinking on his part? It would be far more convenient thumbing a lift than hoofing the remaining distance. "Shall I head it off at the pass, madam?"

"Shall *I* head it off at the pass, sir?" she offered in alternative.

"Shall *we* head it off at the pass?" he

compromised.

Jane smiled and said, "I'm so glad you're not a male chauvinist pig."

"Hey, I welcome company." He was already on the move, and Jane was close beside him.

They gathered their things and re-linked themselves together with the rope. "Whoever from The Facility is in the car will likely stick to the road," Jane decided, "and, thereby, encounter our trashed vehicle cradled in the smoldering remains of *Kenk-lum-ra*. So ..." She paused to let Gerald continue with her thought.

". . . we're better off intercepting them the sooner the better, right?"

"Right," she ran with their combined reasoning, "because in this storm, there's always the chance the approaching car will end up turning back before it ever reaches *Kenk-lum-ra*."

Their shared familiarity with the terrain, aided by their separate compass readings, told them, in spite of the low visibility, exactly in which direction they needed to go. The renewed intensity of the storm, as soon as they re-entered it, cautioned them to reconsider.

It was tough going, and when the road didn't materialize where Gerald and Jane knew it should, their first conclusion was that they'd crossed it unawares; camouflage was a constant enemy to be wary of in a sand storm. They immediately began looking for the outcropping that would be their next official stop should they be forced to go all of the rest of the way on foot.

Jane was surprised when she was pulled up sharply. Squinting hard against wind and dust, she had trouble figuring out Gerald's sign language; oh, she saw his lips and hands move, but she couldn't understand a thing he was trying to say.

Looking beyond Gerald, she saw two ruts filled not quite completely with blown sand. "The road?" she mouthed. Gerald nodded silent assent.

Jane had already given up ever finding it; now that they had, she became increasingly aware that the spot wasn't tailor-made for waiting around for the next bus, taxi, train, or car, the latter mysteriously loosed from The Facility when both the staff and the person or persons on board should have known better.

Jane looped Gerald's strong neck with her curved palms and pulled his handsome face close to hers. Her lips ran the stubble-covered curve of his jaw line to his ear. "This is not ideal!" she screamed doubting even then that he could hear her.

"We agree yet again!" His distant but decipherable voice materialized. "I say that we get our you-know-whats out of here!"

Jane nodded ready agreement as a shock wave from an erupting fireball knocked her off her feet.

The rope cinched tightly around her middle, squeezing her breath from her as she made jarring contact with hard ground.

In the dust to her left, an expanding globe of phosphorescence was still visible, its brilliance heightened by shadows of flying debris bursting past her and disappearing into the windy vortex about them.

"Gerald!" Jane breathed dirt and heat. Her eyes hurt more from the flash than from the burst of lightning that had felled *Kenk-lum-ra* before them.

There was an ominous *thud*, and a flaming tire, reeking of burning rubber, appeared from nowhere and plopped down less than a yard in front of her. A piece of partially melted car fender plowed the sand so close to her that Jane could feel the heat emanating from its bubbling metal surface. More solid objects followed, raining down only to reveal the faint outline of a crater about twenty feet to her left on the wind-blown landscape.

Knowing she was dazed didn't improve her disposition. Nor did the weight suddenly on top of her, threatening to steal away what little breathable air the suffocating storm so stingily allowed her.

"Down, Jane! Down!" It was dialogue straight from a first-grade primer: substitute "run" for "down" and "Spot" for "Jane."

There was a *zing* and a high-pitched *whine*. The

sounds concluded in a ground-shaking eruption that raised stinging sand in exploding coronets, much like those picturesque drops of milk in special slow-motion photography television commercials that hit a countertop and exploded into regal crowns.

Things—metallic, heavy, dangerous—continued to thump and pockmark the terrain.

"Gerald?"

His body was the weight that shielded her, like a mother hen protecting a vulnerable chick. Brave, caring, should-be-concerned-with-his-own-safety man!

A horrible reality dawned in Jane's scrambled brain: if Gerald were hit by any one of these cascading pieces, he and she would likely end up together dead as a doornail.

Dare to Love in Oz

Two

Gerald didn't release Jane even when the crater-making bombardment — finally—seemed over; he feared a late-arriving piece of shrapnel and the damage it could do, returning with even greater vengeance from being flung further into the air. Nor was Jane overly anxious to insist; she was pleased to breathe at all.

The violent thump, thump, thump of her heart was actually reassuring; her mind, temporarily relieved from coping with the terror, tried to begin putting some explanation to the madness.

It wasn't as if it had all exploded upon them

without any clues as to origin.

For instance, the tire: that circle of black, smoldering rubber that had plopped out of the sky like an alien spacecraft crash-landing on hostile terrain; similarly, that hunk of heat-bubbled car fender that had dive-bombed them shortly thereafter. Tire plus fender equal car.

First guess: Gerald and Jane's car, its gas tank finally exploding from the fire generated by *Kenk-lum-ra* except, unless Gerald and Jane's computations were really far off-center, their discarded vehicle hadn't been that near where they were now.

Second guess: the car they'd hoped to intercept.

Gerald's weight shifted, releasing Jane. He helped her to her feet. For a moment, she thought her wobbly legs wouldn't support her, but they came through.

On cursory inspection, Gerald was bleeding. His left shirt sleeve was torn, the material ragged and charred along its edges.

He noticed her concern. "Superficial wound—I

think," he assured her.

That she heard his voice meant the storm raging around them was being deflected, however momentarily, by the crater blasted out of sheer bedrock nearby.

Jane touched Gerald's injured arm; her fingers widened the breach of the savaged material. Blood filled the gash coursing from his shoulder to his forearm. Even if it was really as superficial as Gerald claimed, Jane wouldn't be satisfied until she could examine it cleaned. "You're sure?" She wanted reassurance as if there was anything she could have done if it proved fatal.

"Pretty sure." His skin's responsive jerks, when and wherever she touched, were partly the result of the damage, partly the result of the excitement he experienced at her gentle caresses: pleasure and pain, pain and pleasure. For the moment, inseparable.

"If it scars, you'll have an engrossing tale for your grandchildren." Reflexively, her fingertips found the small crescent scar on his chin; she'd often wondered as to the tale behind it. It was readily visible within the blue-blackness of his parenthesizing afternoon stubble.

He captured her hand in his and kissed her fingertips.

She removed her hand quickly and incisively, wondering as she did how it would have felt to have him linger over her fingertips, then kiss the length of her arm to the curve of her neck. "A car exploded," she told him to divert her fantasies.

"My deduction, exactly. But whose? Our car?" He answered his own question: "We couldn't have been so far off in our directions, could we?"

"I figure it was the car we saw speeding from The Facility." She further suggested: "Lightning?" Granted, she'd seen a fireball rather than the slash-the-heavens bolt like the one that had toppled and ignited *Kenk-lum-ra*, but an ongoing flutter of residue and flame dancing within the dust around them demanded their immediate attention.

Hand in hand, Gerald and Jane approached but were brought up short by a smell that shifted their attention to yet another smoldering tire.

"A car all right," Gerald confirmed.

If further verification was needed, they found it at what remained of Ground Zero. The vehicle, metamorphosing still within a much-reduced cocoon of fire, was, nevertheless, still recognizable for what it was.

Jane spotted something in the sand at her feet and knelt for a closer look. "Melted glass," she identified and looked up just in time to …

"Gerald, behind you!" The apparition was human, its arm upraised and elongated by an unidentified solid object.

The *whoosh* that accompanied the arm's downswing cut a visible swath through the dusty air, tracing a path that missed Gerald's head only by a mere fraction of an inch. Gerald's response was to yell indignity at having been caught so off guard.

The animated manifestation of some cave drawing, half-standing awkwardly before them, issued a low, animalistic growl that sounded both frustrated and menacing.

How Jane went from harbinger to full-fledged participant in the ensuing brawl was impossible to ascertain. She was indiscriminately jerked to and fro, like a puppet on a string, as she and Gerald battled within a complicated and indistinguishable confusion of torsos, legs, arms, feet, heads and hands ensconced in the frenetic embrace of the obscuring storm.

Jane tumbled in a perpetual fog of sand that erased all individual definitions as surely as the succeeding Egyptian pharaohs had exorcised the hieroglyphic images of their predecessors from temple stone.

An unseen hand slapped her hard across the face. She caught the offending hand and, despite its attempted retreat, bit into it, deep and hard, and was rewarded by a scream heard clearly over the continued grunts, groans, sloughing sand, and steady roar of the wind.

She tried to struggle to her feet but each time

was unceremoniously yanked back to the ground, her face pushed into the sand. She kicked, scratched, and summoned all of her reserve of strength; her head however kept being burrowed deeper and deeper, like a proverbial ostrich.

She ate then breathed sand. Her lungs protested, and she tried to cry out from an aching pain so great it seemed to explode within her.

In the end, it was Gerald's better leverage which finally tore her attacker off of her.

Jane took advantage of the moment to breathe deeply of air whose ratio of oxygen to sand, while still irritating, was healthier than what she'd been forced to inhale with her face to the ground.

It was after her gasps tapered off that she noticed the other gasps, close by. At the same time, Jane's right hand closed on something hard that, though hot enough to burn her palm, was enough of a potential weapon to make her grasp firmly on to it no matter what the attending discomfort.

41

Jane's eyes focused on a vague figure sitting astride another, the former's powerful arms wrapping powerful hands around the latter's vulnerable squirming neck. Jane identified the victim not by facial and physical features, because they remained obscure in the shifting haze, but by the umbilical rope that still connected her to him; the cord was the reason why she'd been helplessly jerked this way and that without a by-your-leave. She'd been influenced by Gerald's every move, as he'd been by hers, like two criminals linked by manacles in a chain gang.

Jane reared on her knees and brought the handful of hot metal she was clutching down hard to the strangler's head.

"Nooooo!" he protested so long and drawn out that Jane thought she'd have to hit him again, at the same time aware that taking the time to consider whether to strike him again would have already made a second blow not nearly as effective.

The phantom released his hands from Gerald's

throat only to clamp them to his own lolling head with another loud groan as he tumbled sideways towards Jane.

For the first time, Jane saw his face clearly, instantly recognizing him.

"Ken!" Jane was just as disbelieving an hour later when Gerald relieved himself of Ken Tollin's body which Gerald had ended up carrying through the storm, dumping the man's limp body against one wall of a rocky indentation to gain temporary succor from the continuing bad weather. "I can't believe Ken would do such a thing!" Jane nodded in the direction of the unconscious, discarded body.

"It certainly looks like Ken," Gerald rasped hoarsely. "Blond hair, boyish good looks, five-feet-seven."

"What's he doing out here? Why would he attack us? He worked with us. He's a friend. Was a friend. Oh, I don't know!"

"The only one who knows is Ken," Gerald reminded. "And Ken, right now, isn't likely to provide any answers."

"He is still alive?" The idea Jane might have killed someone, anyone, let alone someone she knew, didn't sit well. She had several valid rationalizations for what she'd done, but those weren't the same as one-hundred percent vindication — at least in her book.

Gerald checked Ken's neck for a pulse. "Alive." Gerald slid down the stony wall, wrapping his legs with his aching arms, put his head on his knees, and shut his weary eyes.

"You must be exhausted," Jane diagnosed. She was dead-tired from carting the gunnysack and water bag; Ken must weigh close to one-seventy. "Take a drink, and I'll take another look at your arm." First aid remained difficult under the circumstances.

"Maybe we should go easy on our water now that we've a third mouth to…"

"Forget it!" Jane interrupted. "And, please, spare me having to tell you the one about the guy in the Gobi with only half a canteen of water. You're doing

Ken's legwork; you get his share of our water."

"You can be so persuasive when you've a mind." He accepted the water bag, took a sip too small to satisfy Jane who frowned her displeasure; he responded with another swallow. "Your turn," he insisted.

She postponed her dig for first-aid supplies to oblige him. The water tasted warm and stale, but it took an enormous conscious effort on her part to resist the uncontrollable impulse to down it to the last. "Now, your arm."

"Don't you want to take another look at Ken's head?" Blood still oozed from the dark congealed mass amid Ken's dusty, straw-blond strands.

"He should have thought about the consequences before he came after us."

"What about your hand?" he asked, noting that she'd wrapped it with a strip of cloth torn from her shirttail.

"My hand is fine." She took a quick peek and decided the two burn blisters, resulting from her choice of makeshift weapon, were broken and well-drained; though painful, they weren't going to kill her—at least any time soon.

"Did I thank you for clobbering this turkey? I was admittedly indisposed at the time."

"Consider it just reward for your pulling him off me while he was force-feeding me sand."

Gerald's wound needed washing. Jane wanted to suggest allocating a bit of their water for the job but knew he wouldn't hear of it, and perhaps rightfully so. Jane sprinkled the gash with more antiseptic powder, noting the blood was nicely clotted. She rewrapped his arm with gauze that turned rose-tinted as fast as she could apply it in the dusting air. "Does it hurt?" Silly question!

"Hmm. I can't say as I've had the time or inclination to notice. Possibly, it does. Yes, I do believe that it does."

Satisfied that Gerald was holding his own, Jane shifted attention to Ken. Her aggressive knock to his head would have most certainly caused a concussion; no matter how well-deserved. The cut to his scalp seemed minor, despite the initial outpouring of blood. Scalp wounds were like that, often initially appearing much more serious than they were. Jane prodded the area carefully, noting a difference in firmness between the undamaged and damaged areas. She thought she could feel the rasping of ragged bone edges against one another. This was definitely not good, but there wasn't much she could say for certain until she accessed the x-ray equipment at The Facility.

Jane sat back and, with Gerald nodding and about to catnap, she addressed her frustrations directly to the unconscious man responsible for their latest mess. "Kenneth Tollin—" He'd once told her only his mother, and people very angry with him, called him by his full name. "—whatever is this about? What are you doing out here? Were you in the car? If so, why aren't you dead? Or were you out of the car? If so, why? And, why come after us?"

Jane checked his head again. She wanted to

make sure she hadn't overlooked anything in anger. Irrespective of what had transpired, she'd be genuinely sorry if Ken suffered permanent damage. In fact, he'd been (past tense?) a friend. He'd offered her invaluable research assistance at The Facility when he'd volunteered highly useful data from little-known studies he'd conducted the year before at Commonwealth Serum Laboratories in Melbourne on tiger-snake venom.

"Umm . . . I'm sure he'll have an adequate explanation." Gerald twitched, emerging from his short doze to watch her. He derived a good deal of satisfaction from the watching.

"He could have killed you." Jane's anger swelled anew. She couldn't put into words the complex flooding of emotions that had swept through her when her mind had registered Ken trying to brain, and then strangle, Gerald. The recollection still made her nauseous.

Since Gerald couldn't fathom, either, what reasonable explanation could be behind whatever Ken had attempted, he didn't press his reassurances. Nevertheless, he'd been exposed to Ken enough at The Facility to know that what had happened here didn't fit the young scientist's usually amicable personality.

"How's our candy holding out?" Gerald thought that a safer subject.

"What do you say to our splitting the 'Peanuts and Caramel?'"

"Sounds like an agreeable compromise."

"Thereby, we avoid stories of two people—" She looked toward Ken and amended her head count to three. "—without amenities, in the Australian Great Sandy Desert, with a peanuts-and-caramel bar they put off eating, until…" She left it there, deciding she didn't like the sound of "they were found half-starved and near death."

When the bar was gone, they split a fudge-covered nougat.

Gerald licked the dusty, melting fudge from his thumb and wondered if his doing so looked half as sexy as Jane cleaning her fingers beside him.

Jane would have gladly confirmed, had Gerald had the guts to ask, that his thumb, mouth, tongue, and everything else about him looked sexy. In the last few hours, since joining Gerald outside Keerborg and foolishly agreeing to running against the storm, Jane had gained more by way of favorable impressions and her feminine insight into who and what Gerald Simms was than she had during all their past years of professional contact.

However, the attraction Jane was beginning to feel toward Gerald also made her uneasy. His inherited wealth made him an oddity in their mutually shared field of toxicology; it was something that Jane, who had worked hard and long for whatever she finally achieved, found disconcerting.

Gerald took a good look at the dusty turmoil still raging all around them. "I wouldn't place any bets on the storm clearing up any time soon. Would you?"

"I don't envy you carrying Ken the distance." It

was her way of agreeing. "With no more convenient outcroppings for rest stops between us and The Facility, I wonder if we shouldn't just wait here until Ken regains consciousness."

Gerald checked his wristwatch. Despite the manufacturer's certified warranty, it was dust-clogged and dead. "The Facility is close; all of us, here, have battle scars that could use further treatment; energy levels are bound to wane as the sun sinks lower; what little's left of the water and candy won't sustain us for long; Ken can regain consciousness and end up as violent as before; the wind could shift, invade this little haven, and send us scurrying in desperation into the storm . . ."

"Whenever you're ready, then." She'd been hoping for a few more minutes' respite. She was a long way from the bundle of energy she liked to be, and for that, she blamed Ken. Battling nature was bad enough without having to battle a madman in the bargain.

Her exhaustion must have showed, because Gerald offered invitingly, "I could use a couple more winks, if that's okay."

"By all means!" She couldn't carry on if he ended up collapsing. In further answer, she felt her eyelids close, her strained muscles melt, and her head drop to the side.

"Except, before I do . . ." He removed the belt from Ken's trousers.

Jane didn't need to ask why or wherefore. A tied-up Ken assured them of rest with less chance of interruption, and neither wanted Ken to slip off without delivering answers.

"Seems a certain somebody left her calling card." Gerald had turned Ken's hand to bind it; Jane stared at her teeth marks, the tissue around the marks puffy and blue. "I think a bit of antiseptic powder might be in order," Gerald continued, "since human saliva contains traces of poison that resemble the toxins in rattlesnake venom, isn't that true?" Actually he'd once presented a paper on the similarities.

"Why else do dentists who work primarily with

children so often fear their little patients will bite down hard without warning?" Jane had heard Gerald present the paper at the meeting. The serendipity of her having been there at the meeting had so pleased her, it made her squirm awkwardly now. She turned to gather gauze and antiseptic.

Gerald's belt finished the effort being used to bind Ken's feet. "Remind me to get this back on me before we head out, or you'll find yourself being suddenly mooned." Gerald indicated the looseness of his pants around his flat midsection.

"Consider yourself reminded."

Jane tried to make herself comfortable. When that failed, she was content to watch Gerald who, scrunched down, looked as uncomfortable as she.

Gerald looked dirty, dusty, tired, and weary. He also looked unnervingly wonderful!

A supper in Darwin, which Gerald had once offered Jane (and which she had politely refused for reasons she knew but he didn't), if now viewed as a reward for their mutual survival, was something she was more and more prepared to entertain. Of course, the idea of grabbing a chartered helicopter to get there (which he had suggested back then), remained an extravagance that still grated on Jane's watch-the-pennies mentality. However, whether she would ever actually accept such an invitation didn't preclude her from harmlessly fantasizing now.

Jane could feel herself slipping between reality and dream—actually having successfully pictured herself across a table from Gerald in the romantic dining room of the Darwin Diamond Beach Hotel—when she became aware of the exhausted, flesh-and-blood Gerald stirring within the rocky depression across from her. Reluctantly, she let go of the very enjoyable illusion to reenter distressing reality.

"Ready?" He sounded more willing than able.

Jane's mind attempted to formulate a response that had something to do with whether or not bears shit in the forest but, then, had second thoughts. "Don't forget your belt," she said, instead, with the faintest of smiles.

As if per agreement, they took separate compass readings and compared results. Disorientation and mind-games were lethal by-products of desert storms; independent verification of direction would help maximize their chances for survival.

There still wasn't a peep from Ken. Jane felt paranoia engulf her as she questioned the meaning of his continued, unconscious state. Gerald, beset with the same thoughts, followed through with a slap to Ken's face strong enough to reveal fakery by anyone except a consummate actor. Jane startled at the sound of the slap. Ken didn't respond.

"Here." Jane handed Gerald a candy bar she busily unwrapped for him. To head off any protest, she added firmly: "You're eating for two not one, now, aren't you?"

"You make it sound as if I'm in a family way."

"Oh pleeeeease, spare me the sardonic wit!" Nevertheless, she granted him a real smile.

He took the offered bar and grinned Cheshire-cat-like while he ate. Finished, he thumped his chest and made a combination of gorilla and Tarzan sounds— Jane wasn't sure which. His chest-beating raised miniature dust storms from his shirt.

Jane only half-faked a cough. "Wrong continent!" she gasped, swallowing dusty grit in the process.

It was time to go. She was glad they weren't delaying any longer; the short spell of dormancy had already noticeably stiffened her muscles. What's more, those muscles got even stiffer as she tried to loosen them. This made reentry into the storm an agonizing ordeal that kept her sympathetic of Gerald, who resolutely stretched, grimaced, and hauled Ken's seemingly lifeless body onto his oh-so-broad shoulders.

Of course, the storm didn't lessen on account of their taking Ken with them, nor did it seem to care that they were becoming increasingly exhausted. It certainly didn't temper its hostility in any way to make their progress easier. Each step was another blind trudge into space seemingly more dust-clogged than before. Dirt danced around them like dervishes in the height of religious ecstasy. Sand chafed, cut, and bruised already storm-blasted skin. Whichever way they turned, the wind simply veered from elsewhere to continue blasting them face-on.

Jane tasted and smelled ground long eroded and eroding: it jammed grittily between her teeth; it flew like powder up her nose. It dried, dehydrated, and desiccated her mucous membranes, and it made swallowing almost impossible.

They stopped three times; the last time Jane reluctantly empathized with what looked in her mind like a sea of Emperor penguins she'd seen once in a nature film, stoically facing down one after another blustery Antarctic gale. Jane shook her head to clear the thought, robotically placing one foot in front of the other and continuing on.

On their fourth stop, Gerald unceremoniously

dropped Ken to the ground. Gerald, Jane noticed, was panting from exertion bordering on total exhaustion. Up to this moment, Jane had held firmly onto a slim ray of hope anchored in the mindless mechanics of walking. This time, however, she thought for sure the game was up, and the storm the winner. She handed Gerald the last of their water, insistently refusing his attempts to press it back on her; she couldn't carry Ken. She was glad when Gerald drained the remaining contents. It took a special kind of man to accept reality when chivalrous instincts weren't conducive to either their mutual or individual survival.

Gerald stooped, zombie-like reaching for the discarded Ken; Jane, despite the reprieve, prepared mentally for the inevitability of meeting her maker.

Her glance upward was towards heaven, associating "up" with the direction she preferentially hoped her soul would take, but what she saw "up there" was the sharp outline of a geodesic dome: a gargantuan, pink-stained egg whose lower limits disappeared into a tapestry of interwoven wind, dirt, and drifting dust.

Jane would never have dreamed The Facility so close. Gerald obviously didn't see it even now. Anxious to maximize the effects of the water Jane had sacrificially offered to Gerald for the good of all, Gerald trudged unconsciously ahead on a course that ultimately would have had him skirting and missing their very objective. The only thing that stopped him was the sudden tension on the rope linking him with Jane.

Fearing the worst, he turned to face her and was relieved to see her standing, hands on hips, though he became puzzled when she extended both her arms and pointed upward. At the same time, Jane, fearing the vision might at any moment dissolve, or become once again shrouded from view, shook her open palms at the behemoth rising beside her.

Gerald, though dazed, stared and finally gave her a thumbs-up sign. He then hefted Ken higher on his shoulders and veered right. Within seconds, the party stopped outside of an imposing metal gate. The suddenness of their arrival was anticlimactic, the effect one of cold unwelcome.

Jane dropped the gunnysack and punched the "call" button on the outside next to a dirt-impacted intercom. "Hello! Hello!" She waved her arms wildly in front of a dust-masked observation camera and waited. Gerald waited. Ken, although too unconscious to know it, waited. Chagrined, Jane finally began frantically searching her clothing for the magnetically coded access card she had carefully stashed in one of her pockets at the beginning of their trip just in case they would need to gain entrance without assistance.

Jane wouldn't have been at all surprised if she'd lost the card *en route*; therefore, she was pleasantly reassured when it turned up right in the buttoned pocket where she'd secured it as Riala was driving her to intercept Gerald at Denbook Gulch.

Jane fumbled about, pushing layers of red, hard-packed earth from the casing, finally identifying the slot into which she inserted the plastic keycard. The mechanism sucked up the card with a grinding sound. She punched in the entrance cipher. The card groaned and inched slowly back out, cut and streaked with shallow grooves.

The expected resonant click of a disengaged lock went unheard, but Jane, come this far, gave the gate a hard shove to the side anyway, and it began retracting jerkily under its own power. Jane motioned Gerald with Ken to precede her, and she followed, repeating the procedure at the ensuing door in front of them. The grinding this time sounded as if a massive, thousand-year-old stone door was reluctantly opening, but the door opened and they entered The Facility. Once all were inside, Jane pushed the door closed, relocking it behind them.

"Do you believe it?" Her laugh sounded amazingly close to a stereotypical witch's cackle, made more so by disbelief, wonder, relief, and a whirlpool of other emotions, not the least of which was satisfaction that Gerald and she had somehow made it through the storm together.

"Who said the modern world is bereft of miracles?" Gerald unloaded Ken and slumped next to him on the floor.

"Listen to the lovely silence!" It wasn't total silence, but to Jane, compared to the cacophony of wind and sand raging outside, it seemed as if it were.

For the first time since meeting up with the storm, Jane felt safe from its unrelentingly fiendish attempts to get them. She would have thumbed her nose but didn't want to tempt fate by coming across as overly smug.

"You wait here," she instructed. It didn't take a psychic's power to see Gerald, braced like an overloaded pack animal too exhausted to take even one more step. "I'll get someone." Jane, too, was close to collapse but, for the moment, the rush of adrenaline that had resulted from finding The Facility had kicked in.

She moved quickly but cautiously along the hallway, her common sense warning her battle-weary legs against any rambunctiousness. She traveled the wide corridor at a good clip, her clacking footsteps echoing emptily about her.

The Facility proper, accessible at the end of the corridor via a flight of shallow, ascending stairs, was secured behind another locked door. The reception "cage" to the side, with monitoring "watch" cameras and consoles, was empty: no big deal given that no one likely expected visitors to drop by in such detrimental weather conditions.

Her success at the other doors gave her confidence to try this one. The slot once again eagerly sucked in her card. She shakily punched in the security sequence and was rewarded with an audible release of tumblers. The door slid sideways automatically with a sigh. Jane, exhilarated, stepped inside.

"Hello!" Her voice, hoarse from its screams over the wind, sounded deafening without competition from the storm.

"Jane?" The surprised voice issued from behind

a partition whose earth-tone mosaic depicted the Northern Territory's most poisonous fauna and flora. Dr. Ralph Powers stepped into view, nervously gripping a Browning HP35 pistol which he held aimed directly at her.

Three

Of all the potential greetings Jane might have imagined from the dark-haired, blue-eyed head of The Facility, this wasn't among them. It left her speechless.

"It *is* you." He sounded as if there might be some doubt. "The audio-visuals on all the intercoms are out." He sounded as if that somehow explained the gun-in-hand. "We assumed you'd wait out the storm in Keerborg."

He tucked the pistol into his belt; Jane's sigh of relief was audible.

"When I heard Gerald had made a mercy run to

65

Sylan Springs, I had Riala drive me to Denbook Gulch to intercept him on his way back here. The two of us decided, quite foolishly it turns out, to try to outrun the storm."

"How is Riala?" Ralph looked relieved, at the same time sounding preoccupied. "She's still not taking Leith's death at all well, but you know that."

Riala still blamed Ralph for Leith's death. The Facility director, alone, after all, knew about Leith's heart condition but had ignored it, as had Leith, when the two went scurrying over rough terrain in sweltering midday heat to entrap that damnable snake.

"You say you're with Gerald?" Ralph seemed at less than full mental function.

"He's at the entrance, just inside the access tunnel. Ken is with him."

"Ken Tollin?"

"There's another Ken?" Jane tried to read Ralph's surprise. "Ken's not in the best of shape, by the way; there's been an accident."

"Accident? What kind of accident?" Ralph's eyes bolted nervously around the area, as if expecting enemies to materialize from the woodwork.

"Ralph, what's going on?" Jane realized her own mental capacity was still on hold from prolonged exposure to the storm, or she would have asked it earlier. "What's with the gun, and why would Ken suddenly decide to come after Gerald with a tire iron?"

Ralph frowned at Jane's latest revelation. "Someone—and don't bother asking who, because I've not a clue or hint of motivation," Ralph said, "trashed our radio and intercom systems. Besides which, Diane is missing."

Jane's tired astonishment progressed from surprise to flabbergast.

Diane Helms was Jake Helms' wife and research partner. At the time Jane was taking her holiday at Mrs. Cooper's bed-and-breakfast in Sydney, Diane and Ken had been seeing an awfully lot of each other on the not-so-sly. Jane hadn't cared for it then; she cared for it even less with Diane missing and the second member of the triangle hog-tied at the end of the access tunnel with Gerald.

"Diane and Sally were out checking snake traps," Ralph elucidated. "On the way back, they stopped at Kronaol Ridge. Diane decided to walk back. We've all done it before, so Sally didn't think it unusual. Even with a storm reported on the way, Diane should have covered the distance easily in half an hour, max. It was only after the storm hit, the communications room trashed, that we counted heads and discovered Diane apparently still gone. Or," he proposed, "back and holed up somewhere here?"

The Facility wasn't operating at maximum residency; it would be easy for anyone to find a pocket of privacy for a long stretch. Even with a full contingency, it wasn't considered odd for someone to stay in his or her room or laboratory cubicle for hours at a time.

"Despite all our warnings," Ralph continued, "Ken and Jake insisted upon taking one of the vehicles out to look for Diane."

Jane's mind's eye flashed on images of the exploding car. At the moment, however, she wasn't up to carrying those remembrances farther, except as to wonder at how volatile a combination these two men, Diane's lover and her husband, presented in the same car out looking for Diane. But death-dealing volatile? "Their car exploded."

"Exploded?" Ralph really didn't look up to handling the unexpected things coming at him as fast and furious as buckshot.

Jane took a deep breath and summarized the rest of what had happened up to where she was. "Gerald and Ken could use medical care," she concluded, nodding down the hall to where the two waited.

"Yes, of course," Ralph volunteered. "Shall we ask the others to help?"

"I think you and I can manage. Gerald can walk, but he's not up to lugging Ken any farther."

A lone Gerald met them halfway. The manner in

which his right hand bunched the waistline of his trousers bespoke of his missing belt moonlighting, once again, as rope in case Ken revived during Gerald's absence. "I thought maybe something had happened."

"Something has happened." Jane proceeded to tell him, and in the telling, wished she hadn't hit Ken so hard. There were so many questions that only he could answer. As they came upon his slumped body, it was apparent, though, that he still wasn't about to talk, lying there still out cold.

*   *   *

The infirmary was located on the fourth of six underground levels: storage/security, dining, recreational, infirmary, living accommodations, and on the bottom level, the laboratory. Top-side, honeycombed throughout the dome, were additional research stations, another recreational area, the trashed radio room, and the reception facility.

Sally Falwen was waiting at the infirmary level when the elevator opened for its passengers: "Ralph, are you all right?"

The attractive blonde woman's concern for Ralph, when there were three others in obviously worse condition, spoke loud and clear as to where her immediate loyalties were. Sally's involvement with Ralph had been additional grist for the gossip mill when Jane had left on holiday.

Jane had always had less trouble accepting Ralph and Sally's emerging relationship than that of Diane with Jake and Ken. After all, Sally and Ralph were single, consenting adults; not that *that* assured Jane's seal of approval, if anyone had cared to ask. Her present concern was how much Ralph's affair with Sally would impede his ability to deal, as The Facility chief of staff, with the infinitely more potentially dangerous "other" affair; people located a in glass house might be unwilling to cast stones.

Convinced Ralph was all right, Sally's attention shifted. "Kenny, whatever happened to you?" Jane had never heard anyone but Sally call Ken, "Kenny", and he'd squirmed each and every time. Not that the nickname didn't fit the young man's attractive, boy-next-door good looks. It was more that Kenny wasn't what any colleague would likely ever call a scientist who'd repeatedly proven his worth and reputation in his chosen field as Ken had.

"Kenny came after Gerald with a tire iron." Ralph's voice was mocking. "Jane clobbered him in self-defense." While they situated Ken on the awaiting examination table, Ralph told Sally the rest.

"Oh!" Sally sounded properly chastised.

Jane wanted to take charge of Gerald's physical exam, now that they were back in civilization, but Ralph vetoed that by insisting Jane step into one of the curtained cubicles for him to assess her physical well-being.

Jane, stripped, was a dirty mess from head to foot, as filthy where she'd worn clothes as where she hadn't.

"Why would Ken come after Gerald with a tire iron?" Sally asked from somewhere outside the concealing curtains. Jane pictured Sally's pretty green eyes, all wide, the corner of Sally's cupid's-bow mouth trembling to enhance the dramatic oh-what-is-happening-here? effect.

Some months before, Jane had been fooled by a similar such "act" to the point where she had actually made a promise to herself to never be fooled again by exceptional, movie-starlet, good looks, especially in Sally's case. After all, Jane had known plenty of women in science, she included, who didn't bag their heads. It had turned out, though, that Sally's natural beauty, combined with Sally's all-too-obvious preference for distinguished male scientists, rather than for scientific work, was what finally made Jane label Sally as someone less than serious about the very serious research projects that had brought all of them to this desolate outpost.

Jane had given Sally every conceivable benefit of the doubt, Jane always priding herself on taking time to probe beyond a person's mere outer facade before making a final judgment; the exception to that rule, self-admittedly, had been Gerald whom Jane had early-on decided was tainted by his tons of inherited wealth.

Sally's initial, blatant, please-be-my-friend-and-confident campaign had initially flattered Jane's ego to the point where Sally and Jane had enjoyed some frank woman-to-woman moments together. It had been sheer coincidence that at the very moment their tentative friendship had begun to solidify, Sally, playing the field at the time, made a pass at Gerald who had the professional ethics to deflect it. If not a coincidence, then Jane didn't care to analyze the resulting breech between the two women any more closely.

"You tell *me* why Ken came after Gerald with a tire iron!" Ralph lobbed Sally's question back at her. "And while you're at it: Why did Diane disappear when she did? Why did someone trash our radio and intercom?" While Sally mulled over Ralph's questions, Jane finished her physical self-assessment and concluded that the storm had left her relatively unscathed. Even her burn blisters seemed benign with the layers of dirt and grime removed.

Jane extended the curtain around her towards the entrance to a nearby bank of shower stalls where, during the first few luxurious seconds under tension- and ache-relieving spray, she thought the dirt converting to rich-red mud that finally sloughed off her was going to clog the drain. When it didn't, she surrendered to the pure enjoyment of foamy soap and steamy hot water. She even forgot the blisters on her palm until they began to smart from the soap.

She was reluctant to leave the sensuous cocoon, but her anxiety over Gerald's condition was returning. She turned off the shower; the continuing sounds of water through the intricate system that sucked the water, brackish, from deep underneath the desert , cleaned it, pumped it into storage tanks, then heated it via solarization, told her someone, probably Gerald, was in another of the shower stalls nearby.

Ralph verified Gerald's whereabouts as soon as Jane, with terrycloth robe and towel-wrapped hair, rejoined him; Ken, laid out on a hospital bed, was a patchwork of wounds better revealed by someone's careful attentiveness in washing him.

"He's going to be all right?" Jane's nod back toward the showers indicated it was Gerald, not Ken, to whom she was referring.

"Nothing a good wash and rest won't cure," Ralph confirmed.

Jane looked forward to a good rest of her own. It, and the hot shower, had been among the final, driving incentives that had kept her going when they were in the grip of the storm. She'd since been disillusioned, expecting her return to be accompanied by welcoming hugs in the arms of her colleagues in their people-friendly Facility, not to an environment gone alien during her short absence.

"And Ken?" Jane did care. She just refused to give it importance over and above what it deserved.

"Sally's developing his x-rays. I suspect a concussion. If that's the case, who knows when he'll rejoin us? A few minutes? A few hours? Days? Weeks? *Ad infinitum?*"

"Ralph, what is all of this about?" Jane pulled up a chair and sat down facing him. After her ordeal in the storm to get here, she deserved better.

"If I were pressed to make a guess, I'd say someone wants to isolate us from the outside world, and limit our communications inside The Facility; whoever it is has done a very good job of both, taking advantage of this monster storm."

"And Diane's disappearance?"

"Most likely no connection." Ralph didn't look convinced. The mere coincidence of two of the three sides of the lovers' triangle going missing, while the third was unconscious, spoke otherwise. Ralph gave Jane an it'll-all-work-out smile, flashing pearly but slightly irregular teeth that fit well with his rugged, tanned face. His overall image bespoke exposure to climatic conditions not so kind to the complexion. He wasn't nearly as handsome as Gerald, nor anywhere close to

Ken's picture-book perfection, but there was enough appeal from his warm, blue eyes, thick lashes, and masculine jaw line to explain why Sally had decided, against all seeming odds, to settle down in seeming monogamy to play house with him.

"No concussions!" Sally arrived holding two x-rays for proof. She slipped the evidence beneath retaining clamps on a viewing screen.

Jane glanced from x-rays to Sally to Ken and then back to Sally. For not the first time, Jane was more inclined to see "Barbie"-like Sally and Ken as a more likely pairing than Sally and Ralph, let alone Diane and Ken. Sally and Ken were, after all, the same age, both single, and both strikingly attractive. It just went to show how much Jane still had to learn about the intricacies of the human heart.

Her heart incongruously skipped a beat when Gerald reappeared, his black hair squeaky clean and tousled into damp ringlets from his shower. The handsome face that had emerged from its dusty covering possessed a burnished glow even more mesmerizing than the one Jane remembered at their previous meetings.

Gerald grabbed one of Ken's x-rays in his hand, curving it slightly to inspect every bone and joint. "No fractures." Practical Gerald didn't need a cryptographer to decipher Ken's x-rays.

"How's your arm?" Jane asked quietly, attempting to remind herself and the others, where their priorities lay.

"Yes, let's have another look now that you've cleaned it up a bit," Ralph agreed.

Gerald's arm was toasty brown and covered with silky black hair that, even now, rode a pleasing landscape of underlying muscle. What remained of the dried, matted blood had mostly washed away; what little remained was neatly kept within boundaries defined by the deepest parts of the gash-like cut.

"A mere scratch," Gerald pronounced.

"Not quite," Ralph disagreed, "but something that, thanks to Jane's persistent intervention, probably won't go septic and cause you too much trouble—if it's watched properly."

"How are you, Jane?" Gerald asked, taking Ralph's pronouncement as a cue

"Feeling fine," Jane assured him. Any additional comment was interrupted by the ring of the infirmary phone. For Jane, the ringing was unexpected, because Ralph had so recently said The Facility communications were "down."

"We sent Peter to fix, hopefully, all or some of the damage," Ralph explained, anticipating her question; the phone continued ringing. No one made an effort to stop it.

Gray-eyed and prematurely gray-haired Peter Sils had gained a reputation for working digital miracles, and as being a general, all-around handyman long before he'd signed on at The Great Sandy Desert Toxicology Research Facility as Chief of Maintenance. If anyone could repair whatever was wrong, it was Peter with his inherent ability to unravel the intricacies of anything mechanical, electronical, or electrical.

Sally was nearest the ringing phone, and she finally answered it. "Peter says he's managed to free some of the inner-Facility phone lines, but the public address system and visual displays aren't going to be nearly as easily repaired," she reported.

"Sally," Ralph instructed, "ask Peter to come down here and join us."

Up until two months ago, there had been seventeen people in residence; four teams, who'd been working in tandem on a project, had finished and pulled up stakes. Three new scientists were due at the month's end. The Facility had capacity for twenty-two people without straining available resources or supply lines. It currently housed six, not counting those who were missing.

"Attention, please!" Ralph requested when everyone was finally present. "We're all here to find out the latest, so I think we can benefit from each other's input."

The unanimous consensus of the group was voiced by Sally: "I vote for crimes of passion."

"Indeed!" obliged Peter. His voice and look chastised Ralph whom the majority thought could and should have aborted the catastrophe at its outset. Ralph's latest oversight only acted to reinforce their collective but unspoken opinion that their leader should have been more observant, too, in the matter of Leith Murphy's fatal overexertion. Peter had been especially fond of Riala's brother who was the only one who had never been too busy to join Peter on many of the major repair projects ongoing around The Facility. It had nonetheless taken Jane a long time to admit to herself that Leith wouldn't likely have taken Ralph's advice for caution, even if Ralph had given it.

It was generally agreed that, what with Diane missing from her walk, her husband, Jake, missing in the car explosion, and Ken strapped unconscious like a lunatic to a hospital bed, there was no immediate danger to innocent bystanders; Jane and Gerald had merely been unlucky enough to stumble upon Ken when he'd "done away with" Jake (i.e. his lover's husband), Gerald and Jane having become inadvertent witnesses to the murder.

The scenario would actually have played better had it been Jake who, after killing his unfaithful wife on her walk, had done away with his wife's lover, Ken, by exploding him in the car. Maybe Ken would oblige with the specifics when he revived, if he revived, though that was becoming more unlikely with each passing hour. Even if he did regain consciousness, having been caught in the act and detained, he'd most likely feign innocence; amnesia was another option.

"I only wish Ken hadn't been so clever about gumming up The Facility communications," Peter complained. "It'll take me forever to clean up this mess!"

At Ralph's suggestion, a schedule was worked out whereby they'd take turns monitoring Ken's vital signs throughout the night.

By the time Jane got to her room and bed, so often fantasized during the last few hours, the combination of arrival, shower, and a pacified, if not fully appeased, stomach (she'd had to eat lightly), left her primed for a long, deep sleep.

She fell asleep the second her head hit the pillow and stayed conked out until her phone rang. Reflexes, honed by her recent exposure to danger, brought her quickly to consciousness, complete with the bad aftertaste of a dream unremembered except for it not being good.

She focused her eyes on the early-morning readout of her bedside clock; the phone rang again.

"Jane Mylor": a business-like answer emerged automatically before she realized it. Who else would someone expect to answer her particular line at this particular hour of the morning?

Jane could barely make out a series of broken whispers: "Someone's here . . . in the infirmary." Jane's mind struggled to grasp what she was hearing. "He's turned out the lights."

The whispers were definitely a woman's, and

84

this narrowed the field to Sally, unless Diane had miraculously reappeared from wherever it was her jealous husband (or Ken?), (or the storm?), (or just the unpredictable Australian outback?), had so securely put her.

"I'm . . . afraid," continued the low voice. "I tried to call Ralph, but he doesn't answer." The sentence wavered as if the speaker were looking furtively this way and that.

"I'll get someone, and we'll be right down," Jane promised. She already had her slippers on and was reaching for her robe.

Jane dialed Gerald. He answered on the second ring, sounding as sleepy as she had felt.

"It's Jane." She didn't give him time for any, *How nice!* or *What can you possibly want at this hour?* "Sally called me from the infirmary. She seems to be in some sort of trouble there, and she can't get hold of Ralph."

"Hold tight!" Gerald was suddenly awake and

on the offensive. "I'll pick you up on the way."

Jane dialed Ralph and let it ring until she heard Gerald's knock on her door.

Gerald wore pants and a shirt, but the latter was unbuttoned and partially opened along the length of his well-muscled chest; his feet were bare.

Jane would have preferred to have more on than her robe and slippers, but there wasn't time.

"How long has it been since Sally called?" Gerald asked without waiting for Jane to speak. They were already in the hallway, the elevator immediately ahead.

"Just minutes."

Gerald didn't summon the elevator but instead detoured towards the stairs. Jane, close on his heels, kicked off her floppy slippers after deciding they would at best prove a hindrance.

One flight up, they faced the door that accessed the infirmary. Gerald didn't immediately push through. Instead, he stretched, marking the position of the protective light screen that dropped around the lit hallway bulb perched at the usual spot on the wall.

He searched his pocket for some protection against the hot bulb. Coming up empty-handed, he started to remove his shirt, obviously planning to tear a piece from it.

"I've a handkerchief," Jane volunteered.

"Keep to one side." It seemed quiet on the other side of the closed door. Maybe his warning was superfluous, but Gerald didn't know what was going on in there, and he didn't want Jane to be any more exposed than necessary. He wrapped his hand in her hanky, waited until she was safely positioned just behind him to one side of the door, tapped the light screen free and then partially unscrewed the light.

It was suddenly so dark neither could see the other, just the faint almost imaginary outline of a door knob before them. Jane didn't like the intimidating inkiness, even if shared with Gerald. She would have liked some—any—indication, if just the pale illumination of a watch dial, to tell her she hadn't been struck permanently blind.

She heard the fire door click open and groan as Gerald forced it wider. At the same instant, she saw a pointed flash of light and heard an explosion of a weapon discharging a bullet somewhere into the darkness. The sound echoed; the bullet ricocheted off something nearby, and that echoed, too. Glass shattered about them like wind chimes.

"Gerald?" Jane's voice cracked in the asking. She tried to swallow, but her teeth were clenched, her mouth was bone-dry, her throat spasming with fear.

"I'm okay," he assured. At least, he thought that was the case. He'd dropped as soon as he'd seen the flash and heard the bullet. The door had re-closed with a loud slam, between them and the danger, under the door's balanced weight.

A flight down, another fire door opened; shoes clacked on the stairs.

Gerald got to his feet and screwed the light bulb

back in.

Peter appeared with Jane's discarded slippers in hand. "What's going on, and why do I feel like Prince Charming after the ball?" He handed the footwear to her.

"Somebody is in a very dark infirmary with a gun that has a bad habit of going off in this direction," Gerald warned.

"Any idea whose gun, or who's using it?"

"Sally said 'he'," Jane obliged but immediately knew the pronoun had probably been generic.

"Maybe we need to put more light on the subject?" Peter suggested. He looked the same as five hours earlier: the same grease stains, the same weather-lined face, the same deep-set gray eyes.

"Delighted to hear you volunteer." Gerald was no coward, but there was no denying that Peter, with his maintenance-man's knack for working in dark places, was better-qualified to reconnoiter.

"Yes, well, there's an infirmary light switch just inside, between the elevators and these stairs," Peter said.

"What say I try for it?"

"It goes without saying that you'll be extremely careful, right?" Gerald suggested. Any less diplomatic warning, he figured, would be an insult to Peter's intelligence and bravado.

"Oyi," Peter said in the voice a popular Australian actor used to amuse American audiences on a series of see-Australia TV commercials. "Now, if you'll oblige me, sir, madam, with a total absence once again of all back-lighting, I'll make my entrance on the completely darkened stage."

Once again, Gerald unscrewed the offending bulb enough to break the connection; blackness returned. Gerald pressed his body against Jane's.

The door clicked open as Gerald gave Jane a short but reassuring hug. As it opened wider, the door groaned; Jane gave Gerald a shorter but more reassuring hug. The door swung shut, its latch clicked once again; Gerald and Jane hugged each other tightly in anticipation.

"We really must stop meeting like this," Gerald

whispered.

"Shouldn't I hear something more original from the fertile mind of a famous scientist?"

"If it takes danger to get us into each other's arms, bring on the danger! How's that?"

Jane laughed in a combination of border-line hysteria and genuine amusement.

Dare to Love in Oz

Four

A sober Peter Sils returned to the hallway, drawing Jane and Gerald back with him into a now fully lighted infirmary. Off in one corner, a frazzled Sally Falwen looked much the worse for wear.

The elevator sighed open and gave Ralph, inside it, a view of the proceedings. "What's going on, anyway?"

"I tried to call you!" Sally accused. "Where were you?"

"In my room."

"I called your room."

"I tried it, too," Jane volunteered. "Your phone rang, but you didn't answer it."

"If my phone was working, which I'll make sure to check, then I was probably already en route here."

"There was someone in here with a gun." Sally didn't sound convinced by Ralph's excuse. "He turned out the lights and said he planned to kill Ken and me. Luckily, I had access to a phone that worked." Her reference to a working phone wasn't lost on Ralph or the rest who were watching Ralph warily.

"I'm sorry," Ralph consoled.

Sally was forgiving enough to accept his offer of a consoling arm and a hug.

"It was horrible. I thought for sure I was dead."

Jane moved over to check Ken who'd been overlooked in the confusion, despite the fact that the gunman's threats had included him. For all Jane could tell, Ken, still oblivious to the world, was no closer to death than he had been, though no nearer to consciousness, either.

94

"Do you know who it was?" Ralph asked, thinking it better if he backed away from physical contact with Sally.

"His voice was garbled, but . . ."

"But what?" Ralph encouraged.

"For some reason, I couldn't help thinking it was Jake," Sally confessed.

"Jake?" Jane echoed. She couldn't imagine anyone having survived the car explosion that Ken, by all prevailing conjecture, had purposefully ignited.

Gerald worked his way through the group until positioned next to Jane; his hand gave hers a reassuring squeeze. Out of the corner of his eye, he spotted the discarded gun. "Our someone left his calling card." He pointed to the weapon lodged against the floor and the wall. "Looks like a Browning HP35."

"Don't smudge any potential fingerprints!" Peter warned Ralph who was stepping over for a closer look.

"You own an HP35 Browning, don't you,

Ralph?" Jane asked, knowing full well that he did. She'd seen it earlier when Ralph greeted her on their return to The Facility.

"I looked all over the room for it before I came up," Ralph said, glancing from one to another suddenly accusing face, "but couldn't find it." He knew what they were thinking. "Do you really think I'd be stupid enough to leave my gun behind?"

"It was dark," Sally reminded. Since he hadn't been there for her when she'd needed him, she seemed temporarily relieved of any reciprocal duty she may have felt to make it easy for him now. "An accidently dropped gun ..."

Ralph looked genuinely aghast. "What possible motive would I have had? Anyone of you could have gotten my gun by simply walking into my unlocked room —and that includes you, Sally."

Jane certainly couldn't think of any motive Ralph might have for terrorizing either his girlfriend or the unconscious Ken.

"I'll play ballistics expert," Gerald volunteered, spearing the barrel of the gun with a ball-point pen and dropping the weapon into a translucent lab bag.

Just in case, Jane verified Gerald's unsullied credentials: "Gerald was with me in the stairwell while the gunman was firing away with Sally in here."

"In the meantime, I suggest we search The Facility for an intruder," Ralph stated decidedly in what appeared to everyone to be an obvious effort to regain trust and control. If he was smarting under pointing fingers, however tentatively directed towards him, his I'm-still-in-charge-around-here voice didn't invite argument.

"Security, as far as I can tell, remains operative," Peter said. He was the one to know.

"Jake had—has—a security access card," Ralph reminded.

"I can re-program the computer to deny him further access," Peter assured.

"And if Jake has his missing wife's access

card?" Jane couldn't help thinking of Diane as dead from foul-play.

"I can re-program the computer to do the same for her card," Peter amended.

"And if Diane is alive, wandering around lost, and finally finds home base but can't get in?" Jane wanted everyone to consider all the possibilities. "I can tell you, from experience, that it's not fun thinking you're possibly marooned out there, just short of safety, at the mercy of the storm. I wouldn't like to think I'd condemned anyone to that fate if he/she didn't deserve it."

"We'll periodically check to make sure no one's holed up outside the door," Ralph said. "Then, if either Jake or Diane shows up, we can let him/her in under armed escort until we can ascertain innocence or guilt."

By the time Gerald escorted Jane to her room, a further search having revealed nothing seemingly out of the ordinary, Jane was too keyed up to sleep.

Gerald opened Jane's door for her and surprised

her by preceding her inside. Curious as to where this might lead, Jane paused only briefly before she followed him in and pulled the door closed behind them.

"Something about this Ken-Diane-Jake triangle waiting until now to go critical just seems a little too pat," Gerald analyzed.

"How can anything be too pat?"

"I've just got this feeling." Gerald would have preferred something more concrete to go on than gut-feeling. "Jake once let drop to me that he knew all about Diane and Ken, and it was no big deal as far as he was concerned. He said he'd always had to 'indulge Diane in her extracurricular activities.' Does that sound like a jealous husband and killer to you?"

"Maybe it does if the jealous husband and killer was merely trying to mislead you with the impression he didn't give a damn, when, in fact, he did."

"Could be," Gerald conceded.

"If Jake really didn't care, then we're back to Ken," Jane reminded, "although how Ken could have been strapped to a hospital bed while simultaneously harassing Sally in the infirmary with a gun is a feat of prestidigitation that would bring him some mighty big bucks in Vegas if he ever decided to take his act on the road."

"One thing I do know for certain," Gerald said, "is that whatever is going on, and whomever is behind it, you and I are verifiable innocents, in that we ended up dropping in on all of this unexpectedly."

"I can live with that," Jane agreed.

"So, I figure, we should stick really close for mutual support and protection, until our friends and enemies begin to sort out."

Jane could tell, by Gerald's look and the sound of his voice, that he was serious. "How close?"

"I on your couch, for instance."

"You don't think you're overreacting?" Jane hoped this wasn't a "come-on." If it was, she had already decided that she wouldn't be forgiving in the end. Their shared adventures had drawn her closer to him than she'd ever imagined possible, and she would hate to see that progress spoiled by his trying to take advantage of the situation. But …

"Perhaps I am overreacting," Gerald admitted; which made Jane less inclined to think him merely out to play Don Juan at so crucial a juncture in their relationship as this one. "However, right or wrong, I'd feel better if the known good guys circled their wagons."

"United we stand; divided we fall?" Jane tried to remember the source of the tired cliché but couldn't.

"If your room is like mine, you can lock your bedroom door," Gerald reminded.

Was Jane blushing? Yes, and she didn't appreciate the sudden flush of color in her cheeks. Her only possible consolation was that it would likely be hard for Gerald to see it through her heavy tan. "I'll get you a pillow and blanket," she proffered matter-of-factly.

She wasn't one-hundred percent sure all this was called for, but there was no denying the disturbing and peculiar "things" afoot. Even if it all boiled down to repercussions from a lovers' quarrel, innocents were being caught in the crossfire, as Gerald and Jane, victims of Ken's attack, had already found out. "Better safe than sorry," she dropped another cliché, but it, too, fit the bill.

When Jane returned with his bedding, Gerald had her framed photo of her with Riala and Leith Murphy in hand. Jane kept the photo propped up among other mementos on a sideboard. The picture had been taken the second time Riala had visited Leith at The Facility after Jane's own arrival there. Even then, the three had been well on their way to becoming fast friends.

"Leith was special to you, yes?" It had been Jane's involvement with Leith that had, not all that long ago, forced Gerald to analyze his own feelings toward Jane. Gerald's need for further analysis was being stimulated by how often lately they'd been near permanent separation because of the near death of one or the other.

"Leith was a very special friend," Jane admitted. How often people tended to misconstrue a friendship between a man and a woman as something different from simply that; as if friendship wasn't worthy enough, in and of itself.

Gerald needed to press on. Answers had become important to him. "Leith asked you to marry him, didn't he?"

"Marry him?" Jane's tone should have told Gerald just how far off the mark his comment was. Looking told her Gerald, however, expected more. "Who said Leith ever asked me to marry him?"

Gerald could have said he didn't remember, but he'd never been comfortable with lies. "I'd rather not say."

"Sally!" Jane perceptively accused.

"Why would Sally think so?" It seemed more than coincidence to Gerald, though, that Jane had grabbed the right name right out of the air from a mental list that, while admittedly not that long, did include numerous other possibilities.

"Oh, it *was* Sally!" The certainty in her voice

provided a final vindication for deciding, once and for all, that she had never liked the woman.

Jane deposited the blanket and pillow on the couch with a fix-your-own- bed finality. Then she asked herself why she allowed herself to become upset over something Sally had or hadn't garbled.

"The subject of marriage, as I remember, came up only once with Leith, and not by way of his proposing to me," Jane elucidated. "It was Leith waxing whimsical as to how he envied people who were happily married and who led normal lives. How could I have known his heart condition precluded any normal long-time husband-wife relationship for him? My reply: 'The right woman is bound to come along for you some day.' Obviously, big-eared Sally made that into something more interesting."

"I'm sorry." Gerald was, too: that Leith was dead, so young, without the right woman ever coming along; that Jane had lost a good friend; that Riala, angered, hadn't been back to The Facility since her brother's death; that Ralph was made, maybe rightly, maybe wrongly, the scapegoat for that tragedy. "It's really none of my business." This wasn't quite true, as he'd come to see it. "Except, of course, I'm interested in everything about you."

"Really? Whatever for?" Jane sounded as if fishing but was genuinely surprised by his admission. There was no denying that more existed, by way of a relationship, between Gerald and her, than had before she'd hitched that fateful ride with him to outrace the storm. There was no denying their new rapport held them in good stead, as far as the unusual—to say the least—state of affairs that had greeted them at The Facility upon their return. However . . .

Gerald wondered if he could put his feelings into words. Maybe he could if Jane would let him progress at his own speed, and in his own roundabout manner. "Tell me about your holiday in Sydney, before you stopped off in Keerborg to see Riala," he requested. "Stayed with Mrs. Cooper, an old friend of your mother, didn't you?"

If Jane was curious by this sudden veering, she was relieved to follow him on it, rather than into more dangerous "emotional waters." "How did you know Mrs. Cooper was an old friend of my mother?"

"Didn't you mention it before you flew out?"

"I don't know," Jane pondered. "Did I?"

Gerald shrugged. Why shouldn't she know he'd made it a point to find out?

Jane ordered herself to come off the defensive, determined to overcome whatever inexplicable "something" that had put her there. "My mother and Mrs. Cooper knew each other before we emigrated to the States."

"You were born somewhere around here though, right?" Then, as if the additional information had been received via ESP, Gerald added, "Tennant Creek?"

Why was Jane surprised he knew? She shouldn't be. Though she'd never broadcasted her past, she'd also never made a secret of it either. Besides, she'd imparted a number of "personal" things to Sally during their earlier, chummier days. "Give the man a Kewpie!"

"Been back there?"

"To the old homestead? Heavens, no!"

"I just thought—you know—roots and all."

Jane saw how Gerald might view her adamant response as somehow unusual. A native-born Aussie, returned, all of these years later, deliberately skipping her birthplace? The explanation, however, entailed a childhood incident that still gave her nightmares, and she wasn't prepared to go into it if, miracle of miracles, Sally hadn't already told him. "I figure there's still time."

"Not much there, now, from what I hear," he admitted.

"Not much when I lived there." What there had been was one venomous snake too many; although, in retrospect, Jane could possibly—on her more magnanimous days—thank that particular viper for having launched her to where she was today.

"Is there anything serious between you and this guy who was scheduled to pick you up by copter in

Keerborg?" How long had that question been festering inside of Gerald, waiting to come out? Certainly, it had gone unasked during Jane and his long race through the storm; he'd had to respect her right to privacy—then. Now, all such chivalrousness broke down beneath his compelling need to know. "I no sooner was assured you wouldn't be Mrs. Leith Murphy—" although, he remained genuinely sorry how Leith's heart attack had removed Leith from the running "—than I received word you're to fly in with the publicity-shy Cole Wilcott who, in a few short months, has become a legend-of-sorts in the Aussie outback." Not many men, at the ripe age of forty-one, chucked the family's lucrative chain of greengrocers—lock, stock, and lettuce leaf—to fulfill boyhood ambitions of adventure.

"Cole Wilcott?" Jane found Gerald full of surprises.

"Right!"

If Gerald, disgruntled, had come to consider Leith a threat, which he had, at least Leith had fit the mold as far as the kind of man Jane had always made no bones about preferring. Leith had had few advantages to help him get where he was. Cole was another matter. Cole, like Gerald, had been born with a silver spoon. For Cole to get Jane-points didn't fit with Gerald's notion of fair play.

"Is there anything between Cole Wilcott and me?" Jane repeated. "Is that really what you're asking?" She found the idea so unbelievably amazing, so absurd, she almost laughed aloud; the notion was made more ludicrous by how she'd fled Keerborg and dared Gerald and the storm just to avoid the blind date Mrs. Cooper had set up with Cole. "Why should you want to know?"

"Maybe I'm jealous."

At that, she did laugh. That Gerald might be serious was simply too fantastic. "Maybe you're jealous; maybe the sun won't come up in the morning; maybe pigs will sprout wings and fly." She viewed the odds for all three as pretty much one and the same.

"Surely, on occasion, it must have struck you as

odd how I always showed up in places where you were: Jamaica, Belize, Maui, Australia." In for a dime, in for a dollar.

Yes, no doubt about that: Jane had commented upon it more than once — a couple of times in fact to Gerald's face. Not only was Gerald often mysteriously on the scene, but he had the infuriating habit of being forever involved in research projects suspiciously parallel to hers: her "seaweed" palytoxins project on Maui, his stone-fish palytoxins; her sea-star saponins project on Jamaica, his sea-cucumber saponins; her tiger-snake proteins in Australia, his death-adder proteins. Had he been in competition with her for the few available research grants in their shared field of expertise, Jane would have outright resented his focus on "her territory." As it was, on the subject of envy, in general, Jane couldn't help feeling a little jealous that Gerald's seemingly inexhaustible financial resources, from three trust funds, left him immune from the money-grubbing, back-stabbing politicking required of Jane and most of their peers. As much as Jane had always tried to stay out of the hard-fought battles for research grants, it was difficult for anyone, not as independently wealthy as Gerald, to do so.

Quite frankly, Jane had never thought to look for an ulterior motive to Gerald's so frequently "being there." She'd simply viewed his presence as off-handedly "interesting" in the same way she might take pleasure in an attractive, exotic, possibly dangerous-but-familiar animal, prowling her property on a regular basis.

"I made it a point to be where you were," he confessed. There it was: out in the open for her as well as for him to see and make of it what they would. He could tell she didn't believe him. For a time, he hadn't believed it, either. "I went out of my way to find out where you were headed next, what projects you were submitting for grant money."

"You can't be surprised if I'm a little unsure how to take all of this," she warned. If their relationship had ever been anything but purely professional, except with an occasional friendly variation, Jane had certainly missed it; she'd consistently turned down his infrequent invitations to socialize outside their mutually shared professional environment. There had always been something about the man that warned her off.

Surely, he'd not misinterpreted the minor liberties of personal contact she'd allowed him, recently, in the face of the dire circumstances that had persuaded her so graciously to accept the reassurances of his touch —on occasion?

"I took pleasure in having you near," Gerald continued and put Jane more ill at ease, "like I'd take pleasure in a priceless gem, an exquisite statue, or any beautiful piece of art. Suddenly, though, Leith Murphy complicated things. You see, before Leith, I'd never thought of you ever marrying anyone, since you were always so much the consummate professional, totally devoted to your work at the expense of a personal life. Still, your relationship with Leith was one that I could, at least, understand. But Cole Wilcott? Part of what kept me from getting closer to you, all of this time, has been your so obvious dislike of men who inherited great wealth. Cole Wilcott was up to his neck in the stuff."

Jane managed, after a flabbergasted silence: "Would you care to run that by me one more time?"

"You've always made it patently clear you prefer paupers." Gerald was immediately embarrassed by his more-than-slight exaggeration.

"'Patently' makes it sound as if I regularly take a bullhorn to skid row to announce my preferences." Jane tried to keep a sense of humor; it was hard to do. She had every right to set down her standards for a mate and stick by them. So what that Gerald, rich as Midas, was biased, as far as what constituted a good man?

"I've always been curious as to how an intelligent person like you could categorically reject a whole class of suitors solely on the basis of an accident of their birth," Gerald accused. "It seems the epitome of reverse snobbery to me."

"My natural father, Gerald, in case you didn't

know, was as poor as the proverbial church mouse. He sought wealth all over Australia, and, when that failed, he headed to the ultimate 'pie in the sky': the U.S. of A. He died poor. His widow, my mother, found wealth by marrying a very rich man who gave her and me all that money could possibly buy and none of what it couldn't; by the latter, I mean genuine care and affection. It didn't last. Mom's third time, however, was a charm; she married a middle-income man with a hardware store and enough love to share: a good father, good husband, good provider, an over-all good man, good friend, and more than good example by which to measure any man. Does any of that put my feelings into better perspective for you? If not, let me summarize, short and simple: having sampled the advantages and disadvantages of wealth, poverty, and several degrees in between, I know what I want; I see little point in wasting my time, as valuable a commodity as time is for me these days, and as little of it as I can muster, in veering from what I believe to be the most likely pathway to my own personal happiness."

"Do all little girls grow up holding out hope of marrying their fathers?" If it wasn't a particularly kind or original thing for Gerald to say, he couldn't help saying it.

"Remember, please," she reminded, "that I've had three 'fathers.' Eliminate men just because they have one or more of my three fathers' characteristics, and I'd really be faced with slim pickings, wouldn't I?"

"All I know is that I've felt something for you for years and haven't—for whatever the reasons—been fully able to articulate and thereby explore it. Maybe it's my fault; maybe it's yours. Who knows? Maybe it's love; although, I always assumed I'd know 'love' when it bit me. This relationship has me guessing."

Jane's idea of love, too, had always been the struck-by-lightning version, and it hadn't changed as a result of Gerald's "confessions." "You'd think, wouldn't you, that for as long as we've known each other, for all the times we've been thrown together on a professional basis, that if something had been destined to happen between us, it would have happened long before now?"

"But something has happened," Gerald insisted. "Isn't that what I've been saying? It's just putting a handle on it that poses the complication."

"Whatever it is you feel, Gerald—and I don't say this to be flippant, because I am flattered—I don't feel any reciprocal schoolgirl fluttering." Admittedly, she'd had a few fantasies about him in her time, still did, but every woman was beset, on occasion, by such impractical Cinderella yearnings that in the end amounted to nothing at all.

"Maybe that's because you're no longer a schoolgirl," he suggested. "Maybe we've progressed to a more mature emotional level that requires more time before the bell ringing and fireworks occur; like a good breakthrough in scientific research isn't usually accomplished overnight, at least without effort."

"All of this remains interesting, but . . ." It just didn't jibe with Jane's long-held, neat, boxed, tied, and gift-wrapped conception of love—if and when it should happen.

Over the years, her idea of happiness had evolved from loving a good man, marriage, a baby carriage, and a home with white-picket fence, to include a successful and satisfying career. It could only, in her wildest imagination, include Gerald, his money, his home in Palm Beach, his other residence in Palm Springs, his villa in Marbella, the penthouse in New York, an apartment in Paris, and his town house in London, on and on *ad infinitum*.

"Actually—" Gerald sounded less sure of himself. "—I expected to broach this subject in a more piecemeal fashion, but I keep thinking of Cole Wilcott, temporarily downed by the weather but panting to come flying in for you."

"About Cole Wilcott." At least, Jane could put that straight. Although, she'd have to be careful that she didn't give Gerald the wrong impression—that she was doing so because of Gerald's sudden revelations. "He and I are not serious, nor do I conceive, by any stretch of the imagination, that we will ever be." Should she add they'd never even met?

She would have explained how she had raced the storm with Gerald expressly to avoid meeting Cole in Keerborg, but Gerald jumped to his own conclusion.

"Is it his money that turns you off?"

Jane felt more and more put-upon. "I certainly have nothing against money, *per se*, no matter what your misconception. Where would any of us be without it? As far as Cole's money, let's just say that I certainly can think of far better uses for it than his self-indulgent fantasies playing treasure-hunter against the Australian backdrop."

"But isn't that what you're doing here: playing out childhood, albeit scientist-to-help-the-world, fantasies?" Gerald wanted to know.

"I find it more than a little amazing that you should choose to compare my work with Cole's opal-hunting dilettantism," Jane was adamant. She hoped that her tone was relaying the disappointment and indignation she was feeling.

"I suppose this means you wouldn't see me other than in a professional capacity, even though I've put my money to much better use than Cole?"

"See you socially?" Jane couldn't help but wonder where such an unlikely prospect might lead. "I think not." She'd resisted before her impulse to explore what this man might have to offer; she resisted now. To do otherwise would be to set her on a course she couldn't see as doing her any earthly good. Gerald didn't even come close to fitting her long-standing ideal of "Mr. Right."

"Rejection is kind of hard for anyone, but especially for a rich man who has suffered so very little of it in his lifetime." Gerald was only partially joking.

"Rejection is an integral part of life," Jane argued and wondered if the same could be said of the possibility she was cutting off her nose to spite her face. "If we don't all experience rejection, at some time or another, how will we ever get a true conception of life as

119

it really is?"

Gerald reached for her arm and took hold. It wasn't a particularly forceful grip, but it produced a chill that shivered Jane all of the way to her toes: an incongruous sensation, considering Gerald had touched her before with far less dramatic effects. Jane pulled free without making her withdrawal overly dramatic, although she remained resentful of even the temporary restraint and, more so, of the sensations it had created.

"We're all dealt different cards at birth," Gerald said, his black eyes locking with her hazel ones. "In the end, who's the best judge of how we play them: you, I, or that higher power you and I both know keeps tabs?"

"I think any kind of relationship with you, beyond a purely business one, would be a tough row for any woman to hoe!" That summed up Jane's current philosophy in a proverbial nutshell.

With that, by way of her exit line, she turned abruptly, went into her bedroom, shut its door behind her, and threw the lock with a noisy finality that she hoped emphasized the inseparable distance she saw as existing between the man in the other room and her.

At first, she thought he was physically thumping protest on her locked door. Through a haze of sudden light-headedness, and a strangely sticky heat that suddenly enveloped her, she realized the banging was her heart, and the humidity was originating from somewhere deep inside her.

She sat on the edge of her bed and attempted, with cool deliberation, to analyze her condition. It was inconceivable she should be so disturbed by his mere suggestion that they extend their relationship beyond the bounds already expanded by their shared adventures.

What did she find so scary about him and his suggestion? What had warned her, during the years since she'd first met him, and what warned her now, to keep her distance and keep up her guard?

Had Charles Dingergoff, the man her mother had once married for the security of his money, really soured her on any man with cash to spare? Nonsense!

Jane never viewed Charles as an irredeemable stepfather. He just hadn't been good enough a man to leave a fatherly impression. The divorce, in fact, had been surprisingly amicable; Jane's mother, the marriage's failure admittedly as much her fault as it had been Charles', had refused alimony, except for a small stipend to hold her over until she found a job.

Compared to the part Joe Mylor had played in Jane's life (Jane had been impressed enough with him to change her name legally to his), Charles' contribution had, in the end, been next to nothing. To hear Gerald insinuate otherwise was pure poppycock!

Jane disrobed and climbed into bed, satisfied, once again, that her notion of her ideal man had less to do with any past negativism left by a rich one-time stepfather, than it had to do with the need for a whole lot of positivism as had been contributed by the other stepfather, to create within her the necessary over-all sense of well-being.

That Jane had resisted the advances of Merlin

Brather, III, in college, had nothing to do with his family's money; he was an obnoxious, egotistical jerk. And Neis Weller, after finishing graduate school, had been discouraged by Jane, because he had a reputation for loving and leaving, not because he drove a red Ferrari.

Jane pulled her covers over her head, closed her eyes, and wished for thought-obliterating sleep. It eluded her.

In her mind's eye she imagined the man just behind her locked bedroom door: sacked out, as he was, for the night; covered, as he was, by her blanket as he tried to fit his muscular, six-foot frame into the small space available on her couch; his head against her pillow; his tan made tanner, his black hair made blacker, by the contrasting whiteness of Jane's own linen slipcover.

Gerald was not an obnoxious, egotistical jerk, like Merlin, nor a Casanova *poseur*, like Neis. Gerald was intelligent, fun, witty, charming, handsome . . . and, yes, very, very rich.

If Jane genuinely held no prejudices in regard to

a man's pocketbook, then what had decided her, from the outset, that her arranged date with moneyed Cole Wilcott was destined to failure? Why face the storm and Gerald, rather than face Cole in Keerborg? Had Gerald attracted her, even then?

"One . . . two . . . three . . ." she counted kangaroos.

At ". . . three-thousand-four . . . three-thousand-five . . ." she decided the counting wasn't doing what it was advertised to do.

She sat up, fluffed her pillow, and plopped back with such force that the springs squeaked. She listened for similar sounds of restlessness from the adjoining room. Nothing, but then noises couldn't be depended on to travel far, what with all the sound-proofing.

"I don't need this!" Jane had to deal with too much else at present, without Gerald interjecting his personal agenda into the mix. "What I need is sleep!"

Surprisingly, this time sleep obliged although it begrudged her pure, unadulterated unconsciousness by running a series of nonstop dreams of Gerald and her, in one disturbingly compromising format after another.

Jane was relieved, and simultaneously disappointed, when she awoke to find that she was not facing Gerald across a candle-lit table at the Diamond Beach Hotel in Darwin.

She completed her quick morning toilet and made a last-minute check of her reflection in the mirror. She decided she'd looked worse.

Unfortunately, she was no surer now of what to make of her confrontation with Gerald than she had been when it had occurred the previous evening. She hoped he had the aplomb to let it slide until she'd had more time to think things through.

She drew a deep breath, unlocked the door and opened it.

"Sally!" Obviously, this wasn't the person Jane expected to see there. Gerald was there, too; his rumpled state attested to how poorly he'd survived the night. Good, thought Jane.

"I thought you'd welcome the additional rest afforded by breakfast in bed," said Sally with a smile that Jane, no matter how hard she tried, couldn't appreciate under the circumstances.

"Scrambled eggs, hash-browns, sausage, orange juice, cocoa . . ." Gerald went down the list. He seemed unconcerned about what had brought Sally to Jane's door with two trays of food.

"I thought we'd lost Gerald when I didn't find him in his room." Obviously, Sally thought explanations were in order. She looked so fresh and bouncy that Jane wanted a go at making her less so. "Imagine my surprise to find him here!"

"I can just imagine." Jane's I-don't-like-you-very-much tone was obvious, despite how hard she tried to suppress it. She could well imagine how long it would take word to get around that Gerald had spent the night in her room; the pertinent fact about the locked bedroom door completely mislaid.

Sally was conciliatory. "It's so gallant of Gerald

to stand guard over your locked bedroom until you can figure out your friends from your enemies."

Gerald's amused expression asked Jane if she really thought he wouldn't make sure Sally knew the situation. What he said was, "You'd better sit down, Jane, and enjoy the food before it gets cold."

Jane was hungry. Last night's sandwich hadn't been enough when she'd eaten it. She was definitely running on empty.

Beware of Greeks bearing gifts did come to mind, but not for long: Sally wasn't Greek, and the smells of the hot food were too inviting.

Sally ran a hand through her blonde hair. After what must have been years of practice, the result was to give the strands just the right amount of additional attractive body and bounce.

"The phone in Ralph's room really isn't working," Sally informed. "Peter checked it out."

Jane ate more egg, drank more cocoa, and waited for Sally to say something more.

127

It was, however, Gerald who spoke next: "I 'worked up' the gun that we found in the infirmary."

"Worked it up? When? Last night?" Jane queried; so much for him having stood continual vigilance at her doorstep.

"I figured, what with your door locked . . ."

He left the sentence hanging, and Sally obligingly filled the breach: "It's Ralph's gun."

"And it's the one that was fired at us from within the dark infirmary, too." Gerald took a bite of toast that turned his lips sexily glossy with melted butter.

Jane tilted her head and asked between mouthfuls, "At us?"

"I dug the incriminating bullet out of the fire door."

"However—get this!" Sally added excitedly. "The gun didn't have any fingerprints on it."

Jane was piqued that Gerald had apparently filled Sally in before getting around to Jane.

"Fingerprints too smudged?" Jane asked

absently, finishing the last of her breakfast.

"Not smudged. No partials or anything," Gerald revealed. "The weapon was spotless."

"So either our gunman wore gloves," Jane decided, "or he wiped the weapon and left it behind on purpose. Why would he do the latter if not to point the finger at Ralph?"

"You sure you can't I.D. the guy in the infirmary as Ralph, Sally?" Gerald prodded.

Sally made another run of her fingers through her hair. "I just got a glimpse before the lights went out. Someone in black, wearing a ski mask like the bank robbers do in movies. His voice, low and raspy, had to have been disguised. Something inexplicably said to me that it was Jake. But, I suppose, I should have been more together and looked for voice patterns and all." She laughed, ill at ease. "I mean, I am a scientist."

Jane had a few ungracious thoughts about what Sally was, but she let them pass and asked instead, "Why do you suppose whoever it was didn't bother to kill you or Ken, since that's what he threatened to do?"

"I don't know. You saw how dark it was in there," Sally rationalized.

"Yet, you were familiar enough with the layout to find the phone in the dark and call me," Jane reminded. "Not to mention dialing Ralph."

"I was only a few steps from the phone when the lights went out." Sally's white teeth chewed her lower lip thoughtfully.

"He let you dial Ralph, then Jane?" Gerald reiterated. "What was he up to all of that time? Shooting at you?"

Sally shook her head. "He only fired the one shot—at you."

"Telling us what?" There seemed no answers, just more and more questions. How could Gerald hope to figure this out when he couldn't even figure out the scramble Jane had made of his emotional life?

"Did Ken regain consciousness any time during all this?" Jane still saw Ken as the best provider of answers.

"Not a peep," Sally reported. "You really walloped him a good one." The way she said it made Jane sound like a certifiable sadist.

"I think I'd better shave and shower." Gerald, aware of the bad vibes growing between the two women, hoped to avoid any open hostilities which would only complicate matters more.

"I'll check in on Ken in the infirmary while you do that," Jane informed.

Gerald didn't look as if that were a good idea. "Why don't you wait, and we'll all go together?"

Jane was waiting for Gerald to say something about their bargain to "stick together" so she could remind him that he'd trotted off last night, leaving her alone while he performed ballistics tests in the laboratory. Of course, she just knew that if she did, he'd replay the bit about how her door was locked, leaving her safe and sound.

"I'll walk Jane to the infirmary and stick around

with her until you show," Sally volunteered. "I mean, I could have made up the gunman, and done the shooting myself, but I'd say the odds were against that having happened, wouldn't you?"

Jane tried to think of any reason Sally would have had for instigating such a hoax and came up with a big goose egg. Jane couldn't put rhyme or reason to anything lately, including her mutating relationship with Gerald.

"Come on, you two!" Sally seemed genuinely piqued when they hadn't voiced immediate support. "How about giving me the benefit of the doubt, okay?"

"I'll be in the infirmary," Jane decided. What Sally and Gerald decided to do was entirely up to them.

"Fine!" Gerald half-yelled his irritated consent.

"Isn't Gerald handsome when he's angry?" That from Sally who accompanied Jane like glue on the short elevator ride up to the infirmary. It was an observation that Jane would have rather expected from a moonstruck high-school girl; in fact, though, Sally was a toxicologist whose work in her field, while never patently brilliant, had, at one time, shown great promise.

Did Sally, who had once made a play for Gerald and failed, see Jane as having succeeded where Sally had not? Jane tossed her head, not wanting to be influenced in any way by what Sally did or didn't think.

"Surely, you, of all people, think Gerald is a hunk!" Sally persisted.

Jane refused to be drawn out; besides, it was none of Sally's business. Jane was saved by the opening elevator door.

"Yo!" Ralph greeted them from inside the room before them.

Jane coolly dismissed Sally. "You can leave me with Ralph. Gun or not, I somehow feel safe enough."

Sally gave a suit-yourself shrug and was back in the elevator before its door closed.

"How are you this morning?" Ralph asked after Jane had joined him.

"Much better, thanks. How are you?" He looked

more than a little peaked.

"I think I'm coming down with some kind of bug, but so far I'm dealing with it."

Ken was still strapped on the nearby infirmary bed, his color good, his breathing even, his breakfast delivered intravenously. Jane asked after him.

"Stable," Ralph diagnosed. "He could come out any time . . ."

Jane suspected Ralph's accompanying grimace had little, if anything, to do with Ken. "Are you sure you're okay?"

"Breakfast didn't sit all that well," Ralph admitted.

Their greatest concern was always the water, but it was checked daily for harmful bacteria; if its chemical composition remained different from what everyone was accustomed to "at home," Jane would have expected Ralph's system to have long-ago adjusted, considering the length of time he'd been continuously on the job at The Facility. "Have you taken anything for it?"

"Just before you arrived. I'll be better, I suspect, in a few minutes."

Jane moved to the side for a closer look at Ken; Ralph tagged along.

Ken was more thoroughly washed than upon arrival. His hair, as well, was blood-and-dirt free; loose strands had a little-boy way of curling along his forehead like bangs onto closed eyes.

"He certainly doesn't look like a maniac who'd wield a tire iron with murderous intent." Jane dared Ralph, or anyone, to disagree with her.

She glanced back at an unresponsive Ralph and didn't like what she saw. "Ralph?"

Ralph's teeth were clenched, one hand fisted against his stomach, the other hand white-knuckled where it gripped the side of the bed.

"You'd better sit," Jane insisted. She spotted a chair, but it was already too late.

Ralph collapsed beside Ken's bed. Jane automatically knelt down beside him and, in doing so, her hair snagged tightly on something; the resulting pull hurt her scalp. She raised slightly, her hand seeking the cause.

"I . . . am . . . going . . . to *kill* you!" a disembodied voice hissed breathlessly from somewhere above her.

Five

Without thinking, Jane screamed at the top of her lungs. Her piercing cry was followed by another, equally long and intense, making a rack of nearby test tubes rattle.

Her assailant had materialized out of nowhere as Jane had followed Ralph to the floor.

While screaming, Jane was reassessing her odds, surprised that her attacker had taken no precautions to silence her.

She located the offending hand in her hair and took hold of it, making every attempt to pry the fingers loose. She clamped down hard with her fingernails which, although not the manicured talons of a woman of means, were survivors of hard work in the field and, thus, able to each make sufficient impressions.

Her situation was thus far defined by her attacker's reluctance to progress beyond hair pulling and verbal threats.

"Let me go!" Jane was amazed at her progress. The offending fingers, mauled deeply by her nails, were loosening their grip on her hair. This inspired her to renew her current efforts.

Even in her distraught state, she realized that whoever was attacking her must be somehow severely restricted as to what he or she could and couldn't do. It was only after she had twisted completely free to confront him that she realized why.

Her kneeling beside the suddenly collapsed and unconscious Ralph had put her near enough to Ken that one of his hands, despite being restrained to the side of his bed, had taken hold of her hair. Jane suddenly realized that his ongoing threats were impotent, as he couldn't disengage himself from the bed enough to carry any of them through.

In the end, all he wrested, for all of his luck and effort, were a few strands of Jane's hair that had come out by their roots.

"You madman jerk!" Jane accused and scrambled to her feet. She pounded her fists against his arm and chest, brought up short only by his vacuous wide-eyed stare that again reminded her how perilously close he had been to the exploded car and how hard Jane had rapped him on the skull.

She grasped onto the bed rail, breathing hard and heavy. Her scalp ached, her head hurt, she felt exhausted. She'd bitten her lower lip.

". . . kill you, kill you, kill you," Ken mumbled. His eyes, she noted, were unfocused.

"Why?" Jane's hoarse voice was loud and angry. She wanted to take hold of him and give him a good shake. "What's this all about, Ken?"

If Ken had answers, he wasn't about give them up. Instead he looked right through her.

Jane dropped the interrogation; first things first. Despite what she might once have thought, she now saw Ken as no major threat as long as he remained battened down, and as long as she kept out of his way. There was Ralph to consider.

She returned her attention to Ralph. His pulse was markedly accelerated, his eyes dilated, his face flushed pink and sweat-glossed. He was unresponsive to a pinch, a slap, even a sharp probe.

Jane knew his situation was serious but didn't have the faintest notion what was wrong with him.

"What in God's name have you done to Ralph?" she asked the wide-eyed, totally out-of-it Ken as if he could hear her and reply. That was followed up by a more rational: "What could you do, but pull someone's hair while strapped to the bed?"

As much as she preferred Ken as culprit, he didn't fit the bill. If he possessed some ethereal ability to disable others merely by thinking such, he would have used the trick on her long ago.

What she needed was a medical consult. Now.

She thought of Gerald first and dialed his room. No answer. Then, she remembered that she'd left him in her room. Again, no answer. Out of desperation, she dialed Sally. Nothing! Then, she dialed Peter. Nothing again.

"Surely someone is out there!" She dialed several numbers at random. After more unanswered rings, she hung up, frustrated even more than before.

"Now what?" A definite quandary. Stay put and count on someone showing up eventually? Leave Ralph unattended and go locate someone? Presume Ken sufficiently restrained as to pose no further problem? Forget that someone had threatened Sally and Ken, Peter, Gerald, and her, firing a gun in this very infirmary?

Again, she tried to rouse Ralph. Though alive, he was lost to the world.

Jane shifted her attention back to Ken whose

eyes remained wide, fixed, staring, and unresponsive. "If you know anything about what's going on here, tell me!" she demanded.

He didn't tell her anything. He did, however, clench and unclench his hands, as if eager to have at her again.

Ralph's dead weight was too much for Jane to wrestle onto an available gurney, so she left him on the floor, making him as comfortable as she could with a pillow and a blanket.

Intuition warned her away from the elevators. With Ralph down and the hair-pulling incident with Ken still fresh in her mind, her paranoia ran rampant. She could easily envision a Stephen-King elevator maliciously alive, waiting to seal her permanently inside.

She decided to use the stairs and, on the next level down, found an unconscious Gerald lying immediately outside his room.

"No!" She refused to accept that Gerald was down from whatever malady was affecting Ralph. She hadn't had time to put her feelings into perspective in regard to Gerald, and she wanted, needed, that time desperately.

What she really needed right now was a miracle, and she knew she wouldn't get one.

Though reluctant to leave Gerald, there was Ralph down, too, to be considered. It was imperative she find help.

What she found slightly further down the corridor was Peter, also unconscious, lying in a heap.

This left …

"Sally!" Jane screamed.

Sally appeared as if on cue. More surprising, though, was that she didn't appear the triumphant archfiend Jane suspected had cooked tainted breakfasts all around.

Jane's runaway suspicions of Sally's guilt were dispelled by one look at a woman who was obviously not at all well.

"You've poisoned us!" Sally accused. She

staggered, pointing at Jane as if fingering Jane as the culprit.

"I poisoned you?" Jane was aghast.

"You!" Sally emphasized and collapsed to her knees. "Why?"

"You're crazy!"

Jane went to help, but Sally would have none of it and used her remaining strength to push Jane away.

Jane retreated and tried to retake everything into account once again.

"Why aren't you sick?" Sally encapsulated Jane's guilt; if looks could kill, it would have been Jane instead of Sally dying. Sally made a concentrated effort to crawl but ran out of energy and collapsed face down. With what breath she had left, she whispered, "How clever you are, Jane . . . to have managed to poison so many toxicologists."

"How do you know you've been poisoned?" *Silly question,* Jane thought, even as she asked: the same way Jane knew.

"I . . . work with the stuff, don't I?" Sally had one even more convincing claim in support of her expertise: "And I'm the one with the pain eating away at my gut."

"*You* cooked breakfast," Jane reminded, squatting next to her and unable to decide whether to touch Sally or not.

"You can't pass this off as food poisoning," Sally chided, rolling over on her back and staring up, hatred blazing in her eyes, at Jane. "I know you've never thought much of my credentials, but give me credit . . . for a modicum of intelligence."

Sally shuddered. Jane shuddered sympathetically. Someone could have accessed the storage area with its stockpile of toxins, some indigenous and some not, to Australia. Of just the former, The Facility boasted venoms from the Sydney funnel-web spider, the Australian red-back spider, the blue-ring octopus, and the sea-wasp jellyfish. Of the world's top twenty poisonous snakes, Australia home-grew the top ten, and samples from every one of those could be found only a few feet away from where they were.

Pinpointing which, if any, might be responsible for all of this wouldn't be easy. It wouldn't have been easy even with a more finite set of possibilities.

"Why . . . did you do it?" Sally's mind-set seemed one-track.

Jane could see how it looked: everyone—except her—had dropped like flies at almost the same time.

Was someone out to frame her? Or had she somehow missed out on being exposed to the poison?

Jane thought for a moment, then left Sally to hurry back to the infirmary. She had a working theory, deduced from admittedly very skimpy data. What she needed now was a snake venom-detection kit to test her theory, and a drop of blood from one of her downed cohorts, except …

Upon looking, the whole supply of snake venom-detection kits was missing. If someone had gone to the bother of purposely removing them, that seemed to confirm that snake venom had been used.

As to variety, Jane had only her runaway intuition to go by. Even, if by some pure luck, her intuition was right, she would still have to work quickly or risk all victims dead within minutes.

She didn't bother putting on a protective lab coat. She simply dialed in the combination on the lock and walked into the room-sized storage cooler to be surrounded by the myriad examples of death collected in the name of science and research. The tiger-snake venom she had collected for her ongoing research at The Facility lay resting obliquely in a wire rack directly in front of her on the shelf, but it wasn't what she wanted.

She wanted antidotes. At the same time, she was afraid someone careful enough to have removed all snake venom-detection kits would have removed the pertinent antidote as well. On the other hand, without a venom-detection kit to pinpoint the poison, the right antidote would normally be indistinguishable among so many: a proverbial needle in the haystack. So, it might still be there.

She found what she was looking for in a secondary containment box and immediately made a bee-line with it, and a syringe, to unconscious Gerald. She wanted to linger a moment after she'd administered his dose, to assuage her desperate desire to confirm that her guess was right by way of the anti-venom working, but she didn't have time.

She proceeded to administer the antidote to Sally, then Peter, and then she hurried back upstairs and dosed Ralph.

To her side, Ken looked quiet and peaceful. He looked to be breathing evenly. His forehead was cool and free of sweat. Even without antidote, his green eyes flicked open. Their emerald hues seemed reanimated compared to the vacant quality seen by Jane when he's tried to accost her a second time.

"Where am I?" His voice was low, weak. He licked dry lips and frowned, apparently at the taste.

"You were in an accident."

148

"Yes," he agreed.

"An explosion. You remember the car blowing up during the storm? You and Jake were looking for Diane."

"Yes."

At least, for the moment, he didn't claim ignorance or amnesia.

Jane plowed ahead, thankful a window on the mystery had finally swung open. "Tell me about Jake, Ken."

"The explosion," he said and shut his eyes.

"Ken?"

If Ken had further answers, he had retreated back into unconsciousness with them, leaving Jane without any further clues.

"Ken!" she persisted, without avail.

Frustrated, she stepped back. If nothing else, his episode of lucidity convinced her his medical problems were different from the rest. She made the decision to hold off on administering the antidote to him; for those not envenomed, the antivenom could be just as toxic in its own right.

She had left everyone where he or she had collapsed, because it had been easier, and it had saved valuable time, to take the antidote to the person, instead of vice versa. Now, however, she was determined to bring everyone to the infirmary.

First, she knelt down beside Ralph to see if his breathing had improved. She couldn't feel any pulse at all.

"Please, no!" Jane knew that even a completely comatose person breathed; lungs filled and emptied, chest expanded and contracted.

She checked Ralph's neck and shuddered at not being able to find any pulse either.

Maybe Ralph had simply ingested too much poison. Maybe he'd taken the poison too long before the antidote was administered. Maybe, horror of horrors, Jane had made the wrong guess regarding the poison and antidote.

She took a deep breath, and a sob caught in her throat. Leaning alone against the wall for support, she prayed her own sudden weakness wasn't itself poison-related.

She closed Ralph's open eyelids, covered Ralph's face with a blanket, and tried to stand, but her legs refused. She thought she was about to be sick. It was hard to separate nausea, brought on by the death of a man she knew, liked, and—more often than not—respected, from the nausea brought on by a toxin that might have finally turned loose inside her, also.

There was no denying this time that her thoughts were of Gerald who might be dying as well, this moment, because of her botched up attempt at a cure.

Her heart pounded, as she headed—with finality —out of the infirmary, along the corridor, and down the stairs.

Gerald appeared unmoving, just as she'd left him. That scared her. So did her inability to find his pulse.

"No! No!" She refused to believe he, too, was dead, because she had been envisioning how it should be while she was running to his side: she standing guard over him when he came awake to marvel at her cleverness in pinpointing the right antidote from so many; he reaching up to her . . .

After several more tries, she detected the faintest evidence of a heartbeat.

Her sigh was audible, made ragged by how Gerald alive had meant so much less to her just mere days ago. Here and now, she was so horribly worried that he remain alive only because the poison might not yet have had sufficient time to do all its dirty work; he might have taken less than Ralph, thus needing longer to die; he might have been exposed later . . .

She sat on the floor and cradled his head in her lap. A tear splashed on his temple and slithered snake-like out of sight. She traced a line from his forehead to the tip of his nose, over his full lips, along his cheek to his jaw line.

He felt hot to her touch. Tendrils of his dark hair were sweat-soaked and plastered to his forehead.

Despite her concentrated focus on him, she heard sounds from deep within the bowels of The Facility; probably always there, they suddenly seemed ominous.

She wished there was a window readily available through which to see the storm hopefully running its course. Once the usual radio interference generated by the bad weather was no longer an excuse, people would question why communication to and from The Facility remained down; Riala would want to know if Jane and Gerald had arrived safely; the mechanic in Darwin would want to report on the progress of the ongoing overhaul of The Facility chopper; the authorities in Keerborg would want to know that The Facility and staff had weathered the storm. As long as the blow continued in its fury, however, no such questions would be asked.

She made a conscious effort to pull herself

together. She was at the moment the only ambulatory person on this sinking ship; the only one left to stand between her downed cohorts and a killer somewhere still at large within The Facility; a killer obviously bent on disposing of them all in any way possible.

She dragged Gerald down the corridor, then reached up and pushed the elevator call button. The elevator took an inordinately long time in coming. Jane prayed continuously that the killer wasn't in it.

When it noisily announced its presence by opening its doors, she stood and for a long minute peered into the claustrophobic but empty cage. It looked suspiciously like the open mouth of a gigantic bottom fish, waiting immobile for an unsuspecting victim.

Still, it was either use the elevator, or attempt maneuvering Gerald up the stairs to the infirmary, a decidedly impossible task she quickly decided.

She caught the elevator door as it tried to close automatically, reached inside, locked the car in place, and with difficulty dragged Gerald in.

She was breathing hard, and it wasn't just from exertion or poison. She knew at this moment it was from pure fear. If she wasn't careful, she'd begin hyperventilating, and where would that get her?

"Be calm, calm, calm." She recited her self-styled mantra to clear, also, the mental and physical cobwebs. To her surprise, she shivered uncontrollably.

She released the elevator hold mechanism and pushed the button for the Infirmary above.

Once she had Gerald—thank God alive—in the infirmary, she realized she'd wasted considerable time in not having loaded everyone on the elevator at once, and she went back to the lower floor, albeit reluctantly, for Sally and Peter.

Sally was unconscious, alive, but still visibly flushed with a rapid, thready heart beat.

Jane tugged her to the elevator and returned for Peter. He felt considerably heavier or, more likely, Jane was nearing the end of the last of her reserve of energy or both.

While lugging Peter down the corridor, she heard the hum of the second elevator car, adjoining the first, suddenly on the move. Summoned by whom? Headed where? She looked at the panel that told where each car was positioned but which had gone out, along with the sabotaged communications network, and hadn't been brought back on line yet despite Peter's initial repairs.

Frozen, Jane realized she needed a less exposed vantage point. She needed time to pull Sally and Peter out of the way. Knowing that, however, didn't provide her with the Herculean energy necessary to put her plan into affect.

The moving elevator car stopped at her floor, and its doors slid open.

Six

Jane began to tremble, her gaze fixed on the towering specter that stepped through the open elevator doors. "I feared you might go and die on me, too!" There it was, out in the open: the unsaid said; the unspoken fear put into words; the gnawing suspicion that had lingered since she'd witnessed Ralph's death. "Oh, Gerald!"

Her overwhelming happiness in seeing him alive, even if he was a bit flushed, released her towards him with the speed and force of a wrecking ball. Like an only half-mortared brick wall, made even more unstable by the circumstances, he wasn't able, with his new-found legs, to sustain her impact. He stumbled back; Jane and he kept moving from the momentum.

Even as they began losing balance together, his arms were claiming her. His own relief in seeing her alive, after his discovery of Ralph's lifeless body in the infirmary, was a balloon of thankfulness inside of him that threatened to burst.

They collided with the back of the elevator, saved by his muscular ass. His strong back and neck muscles, combined with his stunt man's coordination, kept his head from striking against the wall. He pulled her tighter and burrowed his face against her neck. Her wondrous smell and feel took his little remaining breath away.

"Tell me it's you!" she demanded. She kissed his nose, his cheek, his mouth. Verbal assurances, even if given, wouldn't be nearly enough to convince her.

He was sorry when she at last let up for air. Her kisses, no matter the trauma that spawned them, were just what the doctor ordered. "Who else were you expecting?"

he asked her.

"The antidote worked!"

"What antidote?" The last he remembered, before waking up, was the wave of nausea that had him heading for an anti-acid in his bathroom.

She laughed through tears and kissed him again and again to make sure his lips were real, that he was real, that she hadn't conjured him out of her own desperation.

"Want to fill in the gaps?" he cajoled.

She told him what she knew.

"One little thing:"—actually, he didn't see it as all that little—"What made you decide on rust-snake antidote, out of all the possibilities? Our symptoms weren't exactly unique to that particular toxin. I could name a dozen others that would have produced the same effects. A bit of in-depth research, and I could probably come up with a passel more."

"I presumed there was some logical reason, other than no exposure, for me to have been alone functional while everyone else was dropping like flies. How could the killer miss only me, even if he'd wanted? I mean, besides Ken, whose intravenous feed, I suppose, kept him uncontaminated from the tainted food and/or water."

"You've a natural immunity to rust-snake toxin?" His guess was logical—and, he would discover, a good one.

"I was bitten by a rust snake when I was a child. Remember my reluctance to return to Tennant Creek?"

"The old family homestead." He did remember.

"Not too many pleasant memories there," she admitted, "the worst of which was my waking up one night with a snake in my bed. Not helped by its quick disappearance back into wind-rotted woodwork, and my parents' eventual insistence it was all a nightmare. Oh, they checked for puncture wounds, but what would they know, first hand, of a rarity with fangs like hair-thin hypos? Minor epidermal swelling had already covered over the miniscule wounds. No blood. Out of sight, out of mind, at least for awhile.

"Of course, I was really sick by morning. Tried to call for help; couldn't. Tried to get out of bed; couldn't. Passed out; wasn't even diagnosed poison-induced comatose until the next morning. No venom-detection kits in those days; Dr. Southerland and Melbourne Serum Laboratories weren't around yet. Wouldn't have made a difference anyway as there was no antidote back then. So, when they finally did pin down rust-snake venom, there was nothing they could do. Everyone wrote me off. Even I thought I was dead. I still get nocturnal flashes of the hallucinations of me as a sinner in hell." She shivered.

She drifted happily back into the comfort and warmth of his supporting hug, which he was ready, willing and already able to give.

"So, I'm speaking to that rare one in five thousand who survives with life-time immunity?" he said, genuinely impressed and a little awed.

"It was a very long row to hoe. When I finally crawled out of bed, it was to learn to walk and talk all over again. For two years, I was disoriented; my parents and the doctors thought I'd suffered permanent brain damage."

"Well, you certainly proved them wrong! It took someone with well-tuned smarts to put that and what you were experiencing here together."

"When Ralph died, I . . ." She would as soon not go into what she'd thought. Gerald alive, she preferred that thought and the chance that she had likely also been there in time to save Peter and Sally.

"The important thing, you're no longer alone," he told her. "What's more, we know just how far this madman, whoever he is, is prepared to go." Gerald was reluctant to release her; not only had she saved him, but it was a joy with her cocooned against him.

"I hated the idea of our relationship cut off before either of us had a chance to examine whatever it is." She wouldn't deny it anymore; not to herself, nor to him.

He kissed her and this time she didn't resist.

"Maybe I've spent too many years as a scientist, always analyzing the how and why," she offered as an excuse for waiting for so long to admit the attraction she held for him and she always suspected he held for her.

"The how and why of love are often exceptionally elusive," he reminded.

"I thought you said you weren't sure it was love." She allowed herself a little playful pleasure in throwing that back in his face.

"I'm more certain after having been at the brink of my grave," he decided.

"Or, you figure your biological clock was almost prematurely stopped." She was a scientist speaking. "Don't confuse a resulting urge to procreate for anything more than that."

"If you must handle this logically, Jane, at least be gracious enough to let me enjoy our newly acknowledged relationship in my own manner," he chided. "Quite frankly, I enjoy the spontaneity of feelings that comes without minute examination under a microscope."

"What I want is to make sure we don't get involved in something that has more to do with our presently screwed-up situation than with anything else," she rationalized.

"Ah, Jane!" He was disappointed. "Don't you know, by now, that we're all products of our situations— our environment? What does it matter that it took this screwed-up mess to bring us together?"

She faced him more directly.

"I bet you're thinking," he said, "how you really love me and wish you could cut the crap and tell it like it is."

She refused to be won over by his winning smile and good humor. "Actually, I'm thinking: here's a man charming, intelligent, witty, terribly handsome, rich to boot; in short, the epitome of every Cinderella's dream."

"Why, thank you very much." His smile widened.

"How very easy to succumb to his charm, intelligence, wit, attractiveness, and overflowing bank account."

"Thanks, I think."

"I've lived a good many years without anyone of emotional importance in my life, besides my parents," she said. "I don't want to grab for this seemingly gold ring, like a deluded rider on a crazy merry-go-round, only to find it's not the real thing. I've not compromised in the past, and I won't now, just because you seem the perfect package."

"Do you know how turned on I am to meet a woman I'm convinced doesn't love me for my money?"

She wished he would be serious. "Is this really the time or the place for this?" she finally had to conclude. How often had she criticized a book, a play, or a movie, when the characters irrationally (she thought) called time-out for a romantic interlude?

Gerald, though, wasn't ready to let her go. "There's never a perfect time," he said. "A person catches

165

as catch-can, makes do, grabs here and there. Selfish? Maybe! Foolish? Probably! Unbelievable? No! Humans can be very selfish, very foolish, and very unbelievable when they see something wonderful happening even— especially—in the midst of certifiable calamity."

"You're impossible!" she said but kissed him anyway. Before he could say anything else, she kissed him again to make sure it was as good as it was. "There's a killer on the loose who could, in an instant, make moot all of our talk about a new relationship," she reminded.

"Since you put it that way . . . ." he conceded, reluctantly untangling from the wonderful embrace.

She missed his withdrawn warm, protective arms. She was tempted to return to them, but Sally's groan, from the adjoining elevator car, was a distraction Jane couldn't ignore.

Sally's pulse no longer raced like a formula 500 race car.

"One more rejuvenated life to the credit of our resident Florence Nightingale?" Gerald asked hopefully from the elevator doorway.

"Maybe." Jane wouldn't accept accolades until completely sure.

"She looks alive from here," he insisted.

She allowed herself an ever-so-brief nod; then, without forewarning, she was enveloped by an acute melancholy. "So, why did Ralph die on me?!"

Gerald was beside her in an instant to pull her back into his arms. He ran his hand deep into her hair and pressed her face comfortingly against his firm shoulder. "It's going to be all right." He fully intended to make good on his promise.

An hour later, both Peter and Sally, though revived, were still disoriented as to whom they were, where they were, and what had happened. It was another hour before Jane could sufficiently assure herself that the two could be left on their own.

"Jane and I are going to play food-gatherers," Gerald informed their patients. "We've no concrete proof, of course, but we can logically deduce, especially since

Ken seems to have been unaffected, that the snake toxin was somehow introduced into our food and/or water supply. From now on, we can only safely eat and drink canned food, canned juices, and bottled water."

"But who poisoned us?" Sally wanted to know.

"How about Jake?" Peter suggested. "Out there somewhere, angry as hell not only because of Ken and Diane but because Ken tried to blow him to smithereens."

As logical as Jane found Peter's reasoning, she couldn't help wondering why Jake hadn't hung around to count his intended victims. Of course, if he believed there would be no poison survivors, with Ken still safely strapped to the bed, and the storm still raging, he might possibly think he had plenty of time to finish things up later.

Peter asked Gerald to bring him his Smith and Wesson from his room. Sally immediately pitched in, giving Gerald directions to where she kept her Colt 45. Gerald and Jane both had their own weapons which they had every intention of also retrieving for possible future use. The group already had possession of Ralph's gun, used in the infirmary shooting, so it wasn't that which stopped Jane in her tracks in front of Ralph's laboratory cubicle while Gerald and she were out recovering weapons.

What she spotted was a small cage of three very dead rats.

"Something?" Gerald joined her.

Admittedly, Jane's first horror-stricken thought was that the dead rodents in someway indicated that the toxin that had been introduced into The Facility had been airborne. Other live rats, though, in other cages scattered throughout the laboratory, thankfully seemed to belie that notion.

"Maybe, maybe not," she admitted, "except from a hygienic standpoint."

He jiggled the cage. "What do suppose killed them? There seems to be plenty of food and water. Did the killer test the toxin on them first, or are they merely victims of someone's ongoing work project? Natural causes? Old age?"

"Wasn't Ralph working on that non-toxic 'venom' from the snake that bit Leith?" She knew that Ralph had been doing just that when she had left on her vacation, but she had no idea if he'd continued that work in her absence.

"On and off was my impression. Sally would know, as she was, like always, inserting herself into his work as his self-appointed assistant."

Although a lot of people had questioned just why Ralph had persisted with his research on an obviously dead-end street, Jane had always suspected she knew his reasoning. She figured Ralph harbored residual guilt for not having stopped Leith from scampering all over the rocky slope after that snake in the tremendous heat. Had Ralph somehow been able to prove the reptile's capture of some value—medical or otherwise—he could perhaps rationalize how Leith's death hadn't been completely for naught. As for Sally's interest in the project, Jane suspected the woman out to attach herself to any star that could bolster the woman's sagging professional reputation.

"Well, unless there's some way you figure we can use these three dead rats as forensic evidence, food, or in place of a gun . . ." Gerald replaced the cage on the floor.

"On toward the kitchen!" Jane agreed.

"I make a motion to take along a couple of live rats," he delayed.

Immediately, she saw and appreciated what it was he was suggesting. "To taste our food before we do?"

"And to monitor our air supply," he concluded, "as miners used canaries at one time in mines."

By the time they had returned to the infirmary, they found Peter and Sally improved enough to be more than a little curious about the live rats accompanying the scrounged food and weaponry. A satisfactory explanation made, Gerald and Peter carted Ralph's body into the walk-in freezer.

After they had closed the freezer door, Peter

ventured a reason behind Jake's procrastination in making his appearance: "He slipped everyone poison and then slipped outside to hide. Since I canceled his access card, maybe he's locked outside."

"Could we have been so lucky?" Sally sounded with a definite I-don't-think-so. Peter, in the mean time, had worked out a way to better secure their defensive position within The Facility: it merely required double-locking select doors and adjusting the working portion of the alarm system.

"It's not Jake you have to be afraid of!" Ken surprised the whole lot with his unexpected declaration. Heads turned in unison.

"What do you mean?" Jane didn't waste time. If things went as before, Ken wouldn't be conscious for more than a few seconds.

"Jake's dead! That what it means."

"Then you killed him?" Jane ventured. At this state, she figured it was more likely Ken just thought he'd killed him. "You blew him up in the car, and then came after Gerald and me when you realized we were witnesses."

"Came after Gerald and you? What are you talking about?" Ken tried to sit up but couldn't because of the restraints; no one moved to help him.

"You tried to kill Gerald and Jane with a tire iron," Peter said.

Jane expected Ken to flatly deny it, but he didn't. What she heard was, "What were Gerald and Jane doing out there?"

Jane told him.

"I thought you were terrorists." This certainly wasn't the excuse Jane expected. In fact, everyone was surprised to hear it.

"A few years back, I was doing some research with two Israeli scientists who were blown away by dissidents. It was only luck I was unharmed. I still have flash-backs. When the car exploded, here, I wasn't expecting friends anywhere nearby."

"Ken, this is Australia, not Israel," Jane

reminded. Encouraged by Ken's lucid, albeit probable delusions, her nursing instincts took over, and she felt his forehead and checked his pulse.

"I was close enough to the car when it blew to see Jake inside it."

"Okay, but why weren't you in the car?" Gerald was suspicious.

"The road was browned over with sand from the storm. I was out giving Jake directions."

"And you just happened to take a tire iron with you?" Jane was sarcastic and meant to be.

"I blacked out immediately after the explosion. When I woke up, I spotted someone up and about a few feet away; it sure couldn't have been Jake. I grabbed what was closest. *You* say it was a tire iron."

By Jane's account, Ken would have been better off feigning amnesia. This left more questions than it answered.

"Who would purposely have blown up your car?" Jane put to him the all-important question.

"You tell me, and we'll all know."

"Oh God, this is just too fantastic!" Sally sighed.

"Fantastic or not, you've a problem other than a dead Jake-come-back-to-haunt-you," Ken insisted. "Do you want to un-strap me so I can give you a hand?"

"I think we'd be better to leave you there for the moment," Jane spoke for the majority.

"Come on!" Ken argued. "You don't really think I did away with Jake just because I was sleeping with his wife, do you?"

"How long have you been awake?" Gerald wanted to know.

"On and off. Long enough to put two and two together and see you've got it all figured wrong. I didn't try to kill Jake, fail; he didn't try to kill me, fail, and he certainly wouldn't have decided you were all expendable in the bargain."

"Nevertheless, those seem more likely than, what was it, 'terrorists on the loose.'" That from Sally, and she clearly wasn't alone in thinking it.

"I've also been awake long enough to know I'd have been better off blaming Jake for everything."

Jane appreciated his bit of insight.

"I didn't blame him, though, because it's simply not true," Ken said. "Jake knew about Diane and me from the beginning, and he didn't give a damn. You think I was the only 'other' man Diane ever took up with? You think I would be crazy enough to go off with a jealous husband to look for his missing wife if I didn't know their relationship made allowances for people like me?"

Gerald didn't look convinced. "You're sure Jake was killed in that explosion?"

"I saw him behind the wheel when all hell broke loose," Ken insisted. "There's no way he could have come out of that alive."

"So, who's out there?" Sally wanted to know. The way she asked indicated she, for one, didn't accept Ken's story. "Diane?"

"Diane doesn't have a mean bone in her body,"

Ken quickly defended.

Jane shook her head, figuring he was totally biased; although, she found it hard to imagine Diane out to kill the lot of them. Then again, mass murderers weren't easily spotted, or they'd be out of business far sooner. And the killer, in this instance, had to have had access to The Facility, as well as its toxins, food and water supplies. "It seems to me, Ken," Jane said, "that if you reject yourself and Jake, there's no one left but Diane."

"Do you want to tell me her motive or . . . ?" Ken was interrupted by a loud clanging that gave everyone a start; Jane, still jumpy from the events of the last couple hours lifted several inches off the floor.

"Someone just breached dome security," Peter warned at the same time force-feeding them the alternatives: "We either stay put and wait for whomever it is to join us, or we go to him (or her) while we have an approximate location."

"And if neither of those seems conducive to our

continued health?" Sally wanted to know.

Peter, though, had made his decision. "The main security console will pinpoint the area of breach." He didn't wait for a vote but headed directly for the stairs.

After taking only long enough to grab Jane by the shoulders and insist, with an emphasizing shake, "Stay here with Sally and Ken where it's safer," Gerald followed. Jane wondered at how quickly he had forgotten that she was accustomed to deciding her own fate and not leaving it in the hands of others—even if the "other" hands in question were undeniably capable. Gerald, however, was already gone.

Jane checked her Walther PPK to be sure it was loaded and working before telling Sally: "You watch Ken!"

"Jane, for Pete's sake, be careful!" Ken hollered after her.

Three stories up, the fire door was banging shut behind Peter and Gerald. Jane hit the stairs at a run. By the time she was through the fire door and attempting to work a way through a maze of storage crates, there were no signs of either man, except for the emergency wall lights they'd obviously activated on their way through.

She paused in the security room for breath. The alarm was still ringing, only now it was accompanied by a flashing red light on one of the few mint green screens still in operation; the red pulsation pinpointed a side door at ground level, the next floor up.

Jane calculated the likely routes an intruder would take once inside at that particular spot upstairs. She tried unsuccessfully to activate some other screens that would normally have recorded visuals of The Facility hallways to see if the intruder was loose in any one of them.

Frustrated at every turn, she decided to attempt an intercept in the passage the intruder would most likely take to gain direct access to the storage level below.

Gerald and/or Peter must have already decided to cover the same area, because the emergency lights seemed always to be on in front of her. The storage area, on the other hand, was pitch dark as it usually was unless materials were being hauled in or out.

Jane stopped and leaned against what felt to be a packing case. She conjured an image of the master console she'd seen in the security room, with the red light flashing on it. She reoriented herself, confident there was a light switch ahead. She found the switch, flicked it and moved forward, deeper into the bowels of the storage area, toward a yet more distant pocket of gloom.

By the time she reached the fourth switch, she had the progression down to an art; she didn't even pause as she reached out to flick on another light as she rushed by. She hadn't gone an additional six feet, though, before the whole bank of lights clicked off, plunging her into complete and disconcerting darkness.

Still, she refused to panic. After all, the lights in the storage area were on timers, and The Facility electrical system, like everything else, wasn't working at full potential.

In her mind, she ran through the alternatives:

stay put but don't count on anyone until the problem of the intruder was resolved; call out and hope that Gerald or Peter but not the intruder was within hearing distance; feel her way ahead and risk . . .

The decision, however, was ripped from out of her hands by a vise-like embrace that took her from behind and squeezed her breath away; simultaneously, something clamped tightly over her mouth, and another something wrested her gun hand so sharply into the middle of her back that her weapon was rendered worthless except against herself. Her shoulder exploded in a slash of fiery pain that blinded her brain.

Dare to Love in Oz

Seven

Jane was in deep trouble, and she knew it, even before the low, guttural masculine voice said, "The more you struggle, and the more painful this is going to be for you!"

"Let me go!" The words didn't come out nearly as vehemently as Jane intended, muffled as they were by something—a hand?—over her mouth.

"Keep struggling and you'll end up breaking your arm." In emphasis, her assailant (surely Jake) pulled her gun hand behind her higher yet into the middle of her back, another searing, mind-numbing flash of pain ripping through her shoulder, body and mind.

She tried reflexively to bite, but expert fingers constantly shifted, curling and flattening, counteracting her every attempt. Finally, the hand over her mouth began pinching off her nose so she couldn't breathe at all, and she quickly found herself struggling for her very life with no more success than before.

"You want to know first-hand what oxygen deprivation does to the brain?" her captor warned her.

She shook her head and hoped he got the idea in time. She wasn't sure he did until he finally allowed her to take a long draught of air in through her nose.

"Now, calm down and quit making such a fuss!" he instructed.

Jane had never pictured herself docilely acquiescing to any situation, not even one similar to this one, and it galled her how complacently her body complied with his demands even over the express protestations of her mind.

She waited in vain for him to relax his guard.

His body, fused so tightly to hers, exerted a control over her that would have seemed obscene if it hadn't been more immediately frightening.

"That's better." His voice never progressed above a strange, gravelly whisper.

"Jake?" Again, Jane was surprised at the undecipherable mumble that escaped her lips and his hand.

"Quiet, I said." Her gun hand was wrenched higher yet.

Despite the terror and pain, she thought, *Now what?* There was no way the two could stay like this forever. She listened for any clues of Gerald or Peter's whereabouts, but all she could hear were her and her assailant's breathing, hers by far the more ragged.

Suddenly, his face pressed into her hair, his mouth so close that she could feel his lips tight against her ear. "You're going to keep very quiet when I pull my hand away, or you're going to be one sorry individual. Understand?"

She nodded, but he didn't pull his hand away.

"I need to find Jane Mylor," he said. "You do know who she is?"

Jane was stunned speechless; Jake would surely have known who she was. Granted, the lights were still out, but her assailant should have recognized her if just by her mangled voice.

He gave her a shake that would have clattered her teeth if they hadn't been so tightly clenched in pain.

"I don't have all day, lady!" he warned her.

She nodded without the faintest idea where this was going to lead.

"Very simply, very concisely, and very, very quietly, you're going to tell me where, in this rat-infested, rabbit-warren maze, I can find Jane Mylor in the quickest possible time," he instructed. "First, however, I want you to nod if she's in the best of health."

The best of health? Being held by a madman like this in the dark was exacting its toll on Jane's physical and mental well-being that had been already

186

strained by the last few crazy hours. Nevertheless, she nodded the lie.

"Good." The pressure of his hand slackened, accompanied by, "Quiet, now, or pay the consequences."

"Who are you?" Her mouth refused to work like it should; she wondered if he could understand what she had said.

"I ask the questions, and you don't make your answers louder or longer than they need be."

"You won't get away with this. People are looking for you." This she knew he didn't want to hear. She headed off his liable-to-be-violent rebuttal with, "What do you want with Jane?"

"What do *you* want with her?" he countered, full of surprises and obviously more than a little confused.

"I?" She was flabbergasted.

"Just why is it that you and your friends have this place under siege?"

"My friends and I?"

"What do I have here: Little Miss Echo?"

"What makes you think we have anything under siege?" she stalled and hoped "the cavalry" would arrive as it always did about this time in late-night TV westerns.

"I'm not blind, lady. From the looks of them, two one-time cars, each within walking distance of this place, look as though they've been used as bombs. In addition, no one's answering your front door, or didn't you know?"

"The intercom and radio have been sabotaged," she said.

"Exactly!" His iron-like hold tightened about the person whom he held personally accountable for everything going on.

Jane decided to try the truth, since nothing else had seemed to work. "I'm Jane Mylor."

"Sure, and if I believe that, you've an ocean-view property you'd like to sell me at Ayers Rock."

"I've identification, if you've a light to read it."

"Which pocket?"

She told him and gritted her teeth in expectation

of the obscene production number she figured he'd make of locating it.

With barely noticed slight of hand, he retrieved her identification card and illuminated it with a small flashlight. "Well, I'll be!"

When he let her go, her first impulse was to run and scream bloody hell. Common sense, though, took control. An enemy who'd been so much in control didn't relinquish that control if he was planning dastardly deeds.

He raised his flashlight to illuminate his face.

"You're not Jake Helms!" she as much as accused.

"Maybe that's because I'm Cole Wilcott."

Recent photos of publicity-shy Cole Wilcott were scarce as hen's teeth, but some had made it into the press. Mrs. Cooper had an autographed copy of one from a newspaper article, albeit not a very good one, on her dresser. It had been signed by Cole on one of his stopovers, long after his defection to the Australian outback had become less the cause célèbre it had started out to be.

The man had the right hair color and style, as best Jane could remember. Oh, how she now wished she'd been a little less centered on her own scientific world and a little more attentive to the tabloids.

He looked older than the Cole Wilcott in Mrs. Cooper's picture. Then again, the outback wasn't known for being kind to any social dilettante's peaches-and-cream complexion.

"Cole Wilcott is holed up in Grenpewrie Station by the storm," she challenged matter-of-factly.

"The storm is already clear of there," he begged to differ. "I headed to Keerborg, but Riala said you'd already left for here hours ago. I followed the storm and figured to get here about the time it blew over. Unfortunately, it's stalled with its rear directly overhead and showing no signs of moving on any time soon."

"Then, why aren't you holed up somewhere in the clear?" There were holes in his story, although she was more inclined to believe it now than at first.

"Storm center has actually moved miles northwest of here. This place is now on the periphery, so there was enough partial clearing for me to manage a fly-in."

"Madness!" she concluded.

"That from someone who decided to outrun the storm in a car?"

"Touché!" she conceded.

"Besides, flying wasn't bad above the dust. It was bringing the chopper down through the blow that was the hairy part."

The possible "out" Cole suddenly offered sent a spurt of adrenaline into Jane's already hyped system. "Your helicopter is here?"

"I couldn't spot The Facility helipad, so I put down just beyond a dune at the northern edge of your water still."

There and completely vulnerable, Jane decided, unless, "Anyone guarding it?"

"I'm a one-man operation and have been for

some time," he disappointed.

There was always the chance that the killer on the loose, wherever he was, whatever he was up to, hadn't noticed Cole's arrival, any more than anyone inside The Facility had noticed. If that were the case …

"Jane!" It was Gerald.

"Over here!"

The entire row of overhead lights clacked on. Cole didn't take defensive or offensive action, and that told Jane he was who he said he was. Did he know how happy she was that it was he, not Jake, who had grabbed her? Chock up one blind date that turned up not all that bad in the end.

A few yards away, Gerald was brought up short. "Who's . . . ?"

"Cole Wilcott, meet Gerald Simms," Jane obliged.

Gerald looked uncertain as to whether to aim his gun at the man or leave it where it was. "How'd you get in?"

"I'm afraid I broke in," Cole confessed. "I spotted two vehicles that looked like they belonged in a war zone, and a building locked up tighter than a drum, with no response to my repeated requests for entry. My curiosity got the best of me, and has been little assuaged by the alarm and at least three people out to get me with guns."

"We've a bit of a problem here," Gerald admitted. He wished this competition for Jane—that's how he still viewed this ex-greengrocer—was a little less impressive in the looks department. Granted, Cole was older than Gerald remembered him from what he had seen of Cole's initial just-arrived-in-Australia press coverage.

"I'd like to hear all about your problem." Cole flicked a few strands of strawberry blond hair out of violet eyes to present an even more attractive picture. A bit of outside dust remained trapped within his crevice-deep chin cleft which only gave greater definition to that rugged punctuation mark in his otherwise fine-drawn face.

Jane hadn't taken the time to give Cole the thorough look-see his handsomeness probably deserved. At the moment, Cole, for Jane, remained less a living, breathing man, than he did a "something" to extract them from this nightmare. "Cole brought his chopper with him."

"We couldn't be so lucky! Could we?" Gerald was impressed.

"We can discuss the how and why later," Jane decided. "In the meantime, I say we all fly out and leave any killer chasing our dust."

"How many is 'all?'" Cole wanted to know.

"Six, counting you," Jane did the figuring.

"Six are three too many," Cole disappointed. "Granted, my chopper flies four, plus pilot, when conditions are ideal, but I couldn't risk more than three, total, at a time, until the storm lifts."

Peter called from the distance: "Gerald, I've lost the bastard!"

194

"Well, Jane and I have been luckier," Gerald called reply.

Peter appeared at a run, his stop even more impressive than Gerald's had been. His, "Who the hell are you?" was far louder, too.

They went through introductions which made Jane antsy from the additional delay. Finished, they headed back to the infirmary for a quick confab with Sally and Ken.

What greeted their arrival was an aftermath of disaster: a gun-in-hand Ken no longer confined on the bed but dead on the floor; Sally, sobbing uncontrollably, in a fetal position against a far wall; in between Ken and her, a roomful of tripped medical equipment and shattered glass. Sally's discarded weapon was atop a fragmented pile of what had once been Ken's I.V. bottle.

"What?" It was all Jane could come up with, and it pretty much summed up the confusion of everyone she'd brought into the room with her.

"He tried to kill me!" Sally literally screamed

from across the room.

She came unfurled and pushed her back tightly against a bullet-hole-riddled wall.

"Who?" Gerald asked for the majority.

"Who?" Sally incredulously echoed in obvious disbelief. "Who?" She pointed to Ken whom Jane was kneeling beside, at that moment, confirming he was, indeed, as dead as he looked.

"How exactly did Ken get untied and up off the bed?" Jane asked, as she watched the pathetic Sally try desperately to press the wall behind her, as if expecting its bullet holes to absorb her like tar sucked up prehistoric dinosaurs.

"I untied him," Sally admitted loudly. Then, louder, "Why shouldn't I have untied him? Obviously, he wasn't the killer. He said he wanted to help."

"I don't get it." Gerald shook his head to clear it.

"He got hold of Ralph's gun and tried to shoot me." Sally waved towards the room littered with spent ammunition casings.

Sound-proofing would have kept the noise of the gun battle pretty much isolated within the infirmary. This was why the late arrivals had stepped in completely unawares.

"It was only luck that I killed him before he killed me!" Sally screamed. "Luck, do you hear! I thought for sure I was dead." She visibly shuddered.

Peter shook off his shock and proceeded over to give her whatever he could by way of consolation.

"Unbelievable!" Cole said, and anyone present who heard him had to agree.

Clean-up consisted of Gerald and Peter hauling Ken's corpse to join Ralph's in the cooler, while Jane and Cole attempted to coax Sally away from the brink of an apparent emotional breakdown.

"You look like your pictures," Sally said to Cole in a moment of comparative calmness, after Jane made formal introductions.

Without second-thought, Jane could imagine

Sally regularly reading the yellow-journalism tabloids that Jane consciously refused to scan even when in the check-out line of a local grocery.

Jane decided to take advantage of Sally's moment of lucidity. "Did Ken say anything?"

Sally turned a look at Jane that begged: *Please leave it alone, will you?*

The accusatory stare, though, quickly dissolved with a long sigh, and Sally said, "Ken said, 'I'm sorry, Sally. Really, I am sorry. But unfortunately, you, and a few unlucky others, are in the wrong place at the wrong time.'"

"Why 'the wrong place and the wrong time?'" Jane asked, genuinely puzzled.

Sally shrugged. "He didn't say anything else." She appeared to be searching her memory. "Or if he did, I was too busy trying to save myself to pay what he was saying any further mind."

Whatever else Jane might have learned, and she doubted it would have been of much worth given the source being Sally, Jane's thoughts were interrupted by the return of Gerald and Peter.

The two men had been doing more than just tucking Ken safely away next to Ralph, and Gerald clued everyone in: "Peter and I decided Cole should fly out of here as soon as possible with Jane and Sally."

It was the wrong thing to say, and Jane was the first to let him know it. "You and Peter decided! Both of you seeing this as some kind of sinking ship back in the days of 'Women into the lifeboats first!?'"

Gerald actually blushed through his deep tan. "Peter stays because he's best equipped to keep vital systems up and running until someone in authority can get out here."

Jane would give him that. "And Sally goes, because her gunfight with Ken has left her . . . upset." *Good riddance!* was what Jane wanted to add, but she controlled herself.

Jane waited. When it became clear that neither Gerald nor Peter was any too anxious to follow the lead

Jane was offering them, she prodded them both further. "And Gerald stays because . . . ? And I go because . . . ? Come on, guys, give me some help here! Maybe . . . because Gerald is big, and strong, and an obvious he-man; Jane, on the other hand, is sure to sprain her ankle in any crisis situation, like the usual heroine in a romance novel, she needing all the help and assistance she can get from Mr. Right?"

"Jane!" Gerald decided to try a more indirect approach. "Do you really think we should be wasting precious time . . . ?"

"You two could draw straws," Cole said, endearing himself to Jane more than he could ever know.

They drew straws. Gerald looked distraught until he drew the stay-on-at-The-Facility short straw. He had good sense enough not outwardly to gloat. Jane did her, likewise, best to appear the good—(loser?)—(winner?)—whatever the case might be as far as jettisoning this death-trap once and for all. She squelched the temptation to remind Gerald how his unsolicited decision to ship her out hardly fit with his earlier argument that the two of them should stick closely together in order to cover each other's back.

In retrospect, Jane wished she'd skipped the straw-drawing and insisted on staying with Peter and Gerald. Sally and Cole were just as capable of getting help without Jane on board. However, having committed, Jane was now in the undesirable position of being duty bound to accept that she would be shipped out.

Of course, none of it made an anthill bit of difference when, while awaiting her turn to board, Jane experienced Cole's helicopter erupting in a sunburst of searing heat and flying metal.

For not the first time, Jane, so near an explosion when it went off, was knocked head over heels and flat against an abrasive dune of desert sand.

When she opened her eyes, she'd lost a chunk of time. Gerald, whom she'd reluctantly and with false *bonhomie* left inside The Facility, was by her side, cradling her aching head in his lap, caressing her forehead and cheek.

"The others?" she wasn't really all that ready to hear her own condition diagnosed. She hurt all over. Her ears buzzed a constant static that prevented hearing much of what Gerald said. She asked him again.

"Cole has a head injury, but he's up and about. Sally has scratches and bruises but seems to have accepted it all as 'one more burden to bear.' Think you can walk?"

"I've a choice?"

"I'd be happy to carry."

As tempting as that was, she said, "Give me a hand up, will you, please?"

He obliged.

"I'll be fine," she insisted, invoking the power of positive thinking. It helped when she leaned into the wind that, as before, came at her from every which direction. She took one step, then two, and then said, "Any sign of Jake?" She was back, if she'd ever left, to designating him chief candidate as culprit; although, if that were true, then Ken's final fade-to-black was nothing short of downright bizarre.

"None, and you'd expect him to pick us off out here, compromised as we are like this, wouldn't you?" His words told her that Gerald, too, put the blame on Jake.

Cole appeared holding a hand to his bandaged head. "Damn, my head aches like blazes!"

Jane sympathized. What a mess Cole had inadvertently walked into, when all he'd wanted was a blind date.

There was nothing graceful about the way Cole suddenly sat in the sand. "Made total mincemeat of my chopper," he bemoaned.

"Our resident madman seems to have a penchant for explosives," Gerald remarked.

"Come on, Cole." Jane offered her hand. She was surprised by how much resolution and reserve she could muster when a situation like this one warranted it.

Cole took her hand and looked up. His

attempted smile wasn't entirely successful, but it did wonders for a face already boyishly handsome. "Worst blind date, ever!" he said.

Jane's laugh was blown this way and that into sound fragments. "Let's blame Mrs. Cooper," she told him though it was doubtful anyone understood her.

Sally was already inside when Peter let in Jane, Cole, and Gerald. In Jane's opinion, Sally looked too frighteningly calm and cool; all they needed now was for the woman to step off the deep end.

Back in the infirmary, Cole's x-rays showed no evidence of concussion. "Tell that to the hurt," was his you-have-to-be-kidding reaction.

"I'll give the storm until morning," Gerald said. "If it's not blown over by then, I'm taking one of the remaining cars from the car pool and driving out of here for help."

"You go; I go," Jane put him on notice. "No drawing straws this time. Look what happened when we tried to break up a team."

Cole declined even the prospects of any such ride: "My head wouldn't survive all that bouncing."

"I'm, likewise, staying put," Sally said. "As if it makes a difference," she added in put-upon afterthought.

That decided, they proceeded to implement Peter's newest plan to create a more manageable, defensible, and hopefully impregnable inner sanctum. When they finished, they'd linked barricades on all six subterranean levels with the elevators and adjoining stairs.

Gerald volunteered to stand first night-watch; Jane opted for the second. Ideally, they would have been excused the duty, but the circumstances were anything but ideal, and everyone needed rest and sleep.

Jane needed all of her willpower to respond to Gerald's shakings to awaken her for her turn on the roster.

"That time already?" she asked sleepily.

"Not only that, but I've another dead rat."

That brought Jane around more quickly. "Just

one?"

"Just one," Gerald confirmed. "One too young to be dead of old age, so I conducted a few tests. Granted, I can't be sure, but this being a poison institute, it is equipped to get results faster than your everyday, run-of-the-mill laboratory."

"Dead of toxin poison?" Jane persisted.

"Not that I can determine. I'd like you to review my findings. Maybe you can think of something I missed."

They were still mulling over the results, or lack thereof, having moved to include the other dead rats from Ralph's lab in their experiments, when Peter joined them for his shift on watch.

"I've heard of dedication to the work ethic, you two, but shouldn't one or both of you be in bed, considering the itinerary you'll probably have planned for tomorrow morning?" He checked his watch: "I mean, later this morning."

"We now have a total of four dead rats, all with

no obvious cause of death," Jane said, with not a little degree of accompanying vexation. "Not old age. Not disease. Not toxin. Not starvation. Not dehydration."

"I shall remain encouraged that we still have survivors." Peter nodded toward two live rodents that were staring at them and looking none the worst for wear. "Should we be worried?"

"Perhaps it's just an anomaly, but I don't like it," Jane echoed Gerald's earlier sentiments. "It's something Sally could work on while we're gone."

"So, are you two going to head to bed and let me serve my time, or what?"

"I want to go over one of these test results one more time," Jane decided, her professional pride refusing to accept that she hadn't managed to come up with even one decent hypothesis.

"Better pack a liberal supply of amphetamines to keep you two going on your proposed 'drive in the country,' or you're liable to find one or both of you asleep at the wheel," was how Peter saw it. "I'll scrounge up whatever I can while I'm making my rounds."

When Peter returned, Gerald and Jane concurred that whatever the cause or causes of the four rats' deaths, they wouldn't able to put a name or names to it in the remaining time available.

"Nothing?" Peter could tell the answer, just by looking. "Would that I had been so lucky."

Gerald and Jane's foreheads wrinkled curiosity in unison.

Peter didn't keep them in suspense. "All the remaining cars in the car pool are rigged with bombs on mileage devices that become activated when the particular engine involved is engaged."

"Every last one?" Gerald pressed.

"Every last one!" Peter persisted. "And if the car Ken and Jake drove out of here was so rigged, I figure it would have driven just about as far as it got when it blasted apart at its seams."

"Had he known that, Ken could have made it a point to get out of the car when he did," Gerald mused, but he and everyone else knew that believing that had happened didn't even begin to solve all of the existing mystery. A good deal of the time, Ken had been secured to a bed.

"Think Ken had an accomplice?" Peter asked the two of them.

"What would Jake and Ken have had to gain by teaming up for something like all of this?" Gerald tried to fathom.

Jane's opinion was that, "It's all too convoluted to be just a case of Diane and Ken out to find true love by eliminating her husband from the equation."

Peter shrugged. He didn't have any alternative answers.

Eight

Peter was laid out, belly-up, under the chassis of one of the cars in the car pool, attempting to defuse the bomb attached, when the loud bang occurred.

Luckily he didn't hear it; the sound was completely absorbed by the sound-proofing and cement that separated him from it and from Sally who had made it.

"Sally!" Gerald accused. He *had* heard it.

"Scare me to death!" added Jane. She'd heard it, too.

For Jane and Gerald, the noise of the dropped

packet of supplies had sounded even louder than the reality, the tension of the moment having made their hearing exceedingly more acute. No one, not even Peter, was sure Peter could successfully disarm the bomb; although, he obviously thought the odds were in his favor, or he would never have attempted it.

"I'm sorry, sorry, sorry," chanted a chastised Sally who scrambled to reclaim the last of the provisions meant to accompany Gerald and Jane in their anticipated race to safety.

A glimpse out of the dome windows would confirm that the storm had gone nowhere during the night. In fact . . .

"What?" Jane asked no one in particular after jumping a good six inches at the sudden loud sound of the disconnecting fastening latch on the fire door that separated Gerald, Sally, and Jane from the herd of bomb-rigged cars in the parking garage. Despite her confidence in Peter's expertise, the truth of the matter was that she had been expecting to feel the telltale rumblings of his failure at any moment.

Peter appeared through the opened door; he dangled a bunch of multi-colored wires, of which only he was able to make heads or tails. "Admittedly, a bit hairy, but . . ." He took several well-deserved bows and accepted Gerald's backslap in compliment, the dust rising off his flannel shirt like a miniature desert storm.

Jane provided Peter with a peck to his cheek, which had him asking, "If I go back and defuse another bomb, do I get another?"

"Don't you dare risk defusing another of those things!" Jane warned him.

"I don't think I will," Peter admitted, "although, the kiss was much appreciated."

"So, can we load up?" Gerald directed the question at Peter who best knew the logistics beyond the reshut fire door.

"I don't see why not," Peter consented. "As far as I can determine, the only way any of the other bombs in there would blow is if we start up one of the cars and drive it for a few miles."

Loading immediately commenced, item by item being passed from Sally to Jane to Peter to Gerald in the car. Elsewhere, Cole patrolled the barricaded security areas they had recently established to prevent anyone from sneaking up on them unawares.

"So!" Peter exclaimed when they finished. He shook Gerald's hand, resigned and content with the hand Jane offered. "Is it, 'Good luck!?' Or, is it, 'Break a leg!?'"

"Hopefully, we'll be returning before you know it with people better qualified to get to the bottom of this mess," Jane said. "Until then, be careful and hold down the fort."

Sally passed around her limp hand and muttered what might or might not have been wishes for a safe journey. Jane and Gerald then climbed inside the car, shutting and locking the doors. Gerald rolled down a window on the driver's side.

"I know you've undoubtedly done a first-rate

job with this, Peter," Gerald said, "but I would feel better if both you and Sally were on the other side of the fire door, with it shut, before I start up. If for whatever the reason the four of us went up in a puff of smoke, that would leave only Cole, who got here a little late in the game, to explain all the nuances to the authorities when they finally arrive."

Only after Peter and Sally had complied with Gerald's request did the car start and get put in gear.

On signal from the remote within the car, the garage door slowly began to grind open.

Gerald eased the vehicle through the opening and into the storm, stopping just long enough to make certain that the door had closed completely behind him. No way did he want anyone sneaking up on Sally, Cole, and Peter.

Jane was still breathing excitedly even after The Facility was long swallowed in the blow of swirling dust behind them.

"These are better driving conditions than we're

used to," Gerald offered by way of encouragement. "Granted, I'm not talking clear air and blue skies, but there's visibility beyond my extended arm, and the road is presenting a recognizable shoulder." Jane noticed nonetheless that he glued a periodic eye on the dashboard compass.

The first real indication that things weren't what they seemed came when Jane remarked on how they should long since have covered the distance to the exploded car.

The storm chose that particular moment to regroup as if announcing that it wasn't to be discounted quite yet.

"I haven't spotted any sign of wreckage, but then . . ." Gerald brought the car to a sudden and complete stop.

"What?" Jane expected the worst, unsure just what, of all the possibilities, the very worst might be.

"Dune ahead!" said Gerald.

The wind gusted to reveal an enormous hump of

sand covering what had been the roadway.

The one protestation Jane didn't make was, "It couldn't be!" She had enough respect for an Australian storm by now, and for this storm in particular, to know better. She'd seen the tiny whirlwinds in lesser storms rearrange entire landscapes in seconds.

"Pawnellie Creek," Gerald read her mind. "Nineteen-thirteen. Town of two-thousand gold miners, all traces of civilization created by them gone in an overnight dust storm."

As a girl, Jane had seen where the creek for which the town was named still bubbled out as a small artesian spring in the foothills of Mt. Woodroofe. Less than a mile after it squirted free of the earth, it disappeared into a vast, desolate expanse of sucking desert wasteland.

"I'll check the dune," Jane said. Not waiting for Gerald to acquiesce, she opened the door and climbed out into the biting dust and intense heat. The storm sounds grated on her senses as she closed the door reluctantly behind her.

Gerald watched her almost disappear thigh-deep in the dune and swirling sand. Returning to the car, she reported: "No way over that thing, at least from here."

They turned to drive perpendicular to the sandy roadblock.

Driving the rough proved smoother than expected; not so unusual in an environment where even a few cars deepened every rut and hole in the roadways; ruts and holes that, when filled with blown sand, proved more a hindrance than assist.

They monitored the gas and water, neither of which they wanted to run out. They had a reserve tank of gas, in addition to several back-up cans; there was plenty of water to reach Keerborg, even taking into account any sizable detour, though further detours were the last things they wanted. More importantly, with the dust still billowing around them, they seemed to be travelling but going nowhere.

Their hopes reached a new low when Jane heard

herself suggest, "Maybe if we backtracked . . ."

Gerald's, "Let's try this way a few minutes more," brought them to where they felt their luck had finally turned. He stopped the car.

They got out and walked the top of a crusty, seemingly solid surface. A lull in the storm provided their first vista—one that hinted of visible sunshine farther on. Jane thought she even saw bits of blue sky, but they were too fleeting for her to be sure.

Jane quietly pointed to an insignificant hump of eroded gray sandstone. "Where Leith died," she superfluously identified the landmark.

"Want to talk?" Gerald suggested. The pause in the storm seemed to invite conversation.

"What's to say?" She knew the story, and so did he.

"You were there, weren't you?" He hadn't been.

"Sally and I dropped off Leith and Ralph. They were to clear the snake trap that had been set up there. Sally and I drove on to clear the one at Certtinelle Point."

If it supposedly helped to talk such things through, what was the pressure building behind her rib cage?

"Ralph called you on a walkie-talkie?" He prodded.

"Mmm. He said Leith was dead. That's all." Had Jane ever really forgiven Ralph for leaving it at that? It seemed so callous of him to have continued on after that snake, what with Leith dead and neglected in the sweltering noonday sun. "Ralph later said he couldn't waste time giving me specifics, or the snake might have escaped; a sort of Leith-dead-for-nothing scenario."

Gerald sensed Jane's unspoken need and slipped his arm around her waist.

"'Here, give me a hand!' was what Ralph yelled at me." She continued, "When Sally and I responded to his short-lived bit on the walkie-talkie, I at first thought Leith had revived or something. But, as soon as I spotted his body off to one side, I knew he was gone. 'Help with what?' I asked Ralph. What he had, of course, was the snake cornered, but he'd lost his noose-pole and sack in the process. He didn't want to risk grabbing the snake by hand; he still believed Leith was dead from the snake bite. Why wouldn't he have blamed it on a bite, instead of Leith's heart condition? Do you ever remember Leith acting like a man with a serious medical problem?"

Gerald shook his head; he'd been as surprised by the news as anyone.

"It was probably easy for Ralph to forget in the excitement," Jane was generous. "Wouldn't you get excited if you haphazardly stumbled on a snake heretofore unknown to science?"

"I hear it didn't excite you too much at the time. Sally ended up helping him bag it, didn't she?"

Another reason Jane disliked Sally was the nonchalant way that woman had accepted Leith as dead and had shifted her priorities accordingly. Was it Sally's notion of glory, sharing the capture of that rare, and possibly important, reptile, which had bound her to Ralph from then on?

Jane always thought it poetic justice that the

snake had not only proved itself non-toxic but had dropped dead after only four short days of captivity. For all the good it had done them, Sally and Ralph might as well have let the snake escape and shown a little more respect for the dead. It had been sad the way Ralph, right up to the last, kept working on what little fluid he could milk from that captured reptile. Jane only wished whatever he'd gotten from it, or from any other, had left Sally with nothing of value to pilfer for her own benefit.

"All of that was then," she concluded. "All of this is now."

"So, do we attempt crossing the dune here?" Gerald nodded toward a seemingly natural ramp.

"It does seem the best ballgame in town," she said.

Back in the car, he shoved it in gear and gave its front wheels a sharp twist to best take on the obstacle.

"No one will ever convince me Australia is boring," Jane said as she settled back and wished it more mundane.

The ascent proved steeper than it appeared.

It wasn't so much the sound of the crust breaking and separating from the underlying sand under the wheels as much as it was the way the car, despite Gerald's best efforts to keep its wheels aimed uphill, slid ninety-degrees and would have tossed Gerald into Jane's lap if not for his seat harness.

"Hold on!" he warned, well-advised when the car suddenly dropped onto its side with a bang.

It was like a carnival-ride horror where the passenger cage suddenly locked suspended upside down, loose pocket change raining all about, except, this was more scary: the car continued rolling slowly over and over, side-down, bottom-down, side-down, roof-down, to the constant clang and thud of everything not tied down.

Jane would have had greater cause for concern had her ride lasted longer. After two complete somersaults, though, the vehicle's weight rocked from one side's tires to the other, and then back again, to stop blessedly in its normal upright position.

"Jane?"

She knew that he was talking to her, but she hadn't had time to settle her stomach and take sufficient stock, yet, to know how she felt.

He looked okay, but she wanted proof: "You?"

"Fine, I think," he decided.

Her door had survived with little apparent damage. She opened it and stepped out, genuinely surprised when her legs buckled. She would have gone down if not for the opened door she was able to grab for support.

"Jane?" Gerald feared the shock might somehow be masking some real injuries, and he hurried out to join her.

"Just a bit wobbly," she assured him. "The same happens whenever I ride a roller coaster." A slight exaggeration, but what the heck!

He eased her into a sitting posture in the sand, then went back and tried the motor which had stalled during the roll. When the motor wouldn't turn over, he opened the hood and began searching for something he could do to get the car running again.

After a few minutes, she joined him under the hood. After all, she was more than a mere novice car mechanic. It would have been madness to do field work in the kind of places she'd been without having the basics of improvised engine repair down pat.

Shortly after the two of them managed to get the motor, if not started, at least producing an encouraging whine and chug with each turn of the ignition, Gerald ordered a brief respite and pointed skyward: "Can you believe—blue?"

The cerulean sliver before them expanded and spilled sunlight. The wind stopped and with it the incessant sound.

"Well, it's about time Mother Nature gave us a break," was the extent of Jane's gratitude. Ten minutes later, however, the sun-leaking blue sky had heated the car's metal body to temperatures uncomfortable to the touch.

Jane switched back to practical: "The sooner we get this car fixed, the sooner we get over this dune, the faster we get to Keerborg, the quicker we get help back to Cole and Peter — and Sally. Besides, we have no guarantees the storm's pulled out for good." The blue overhead melded into dusty red swirls at their back and sides. "A change of wind could wrap us back in the sand, and, quite frankly, it's a lot easier working when not breathing dirt."

She was, of course, right. "Slave driver!" Gerald accused anyway.

They were rewarded for their perseverance when, an hour later, the motor finally took hold and didn't desist until Gerald switched it off.

In celebration, they danced.

After rearranging the interior as best they could, Gerald started the motor again; they continued around the dune. A couple of miles further, the dune, now entirely behind them, petered abruptly to nonexistence. Gerald turned the car on the most direct route to Keerborg.

Everything went fine until a menacing section of storm blew back towards them at nightfall, making driving in the dark impossible.

"I could use a quick sleep." Gerald wiggled a persistent cramp out of his toes. "We don't want to get careless from exhaustion or from excessive pill-popping."

Jane nodded in exhausted agreement. She was already drifting, her head on his shoulder, almost asleep, prevented from it only by the amphetamines that continued jazzing her up. Outside and above, stars could be seen, on occasion, through the dust-blown sky on the other side of the windscreen. It gave hope for a clear tomorrow. When sleep finally came, it wasn't the best she ever had. She kept awaking every few minutes to verify that the desert sands hadn't buried them alive.

Finally, she fully awoke to warm sunlight streaming in through the car window. She yawned, stretched in its warmth, and suddenly felt it disappear into shadow. Disappointed, she opened her eyes to see a back-lit human face grotesquely silhouetted against the glass inches from her. She screamed.

Gerald awoke, gun in hand, and Jane realized the face that had appeared, and was now gone, was one she recognized.

She opened the car door, falling more than stepping out. Regaining her balance awkwardly, she did a quick three-hundred-and-sixty degree look around but saw nothing.

"What is it?" Gerald's hair was attractively tousled, his clothes rumpled, his stubble blue-black against the tan of his face.

"Not what; who." She turned, parenthesized her mouth with curved hands and shouted as loud as she could, "Noah! It's Jane Mylor. Remember? Riala's friend."

"Please, tell me we're not talking Noah of the ark here," Gerald begged.

Her smile reassured him that she wasn't crazy. "Aborigine Noah," she elucidated. "Riala's handyman."

He took a look around but saw nothing. "From

Keerborg?"

"He wasn't at Riala's when I was there this last time," she remembered. "His son said he'd gone into the bush on a walk-about quest. Riala said he did it whenever he got fed up with the accoutrements of civilization."

"Well, this is about as far and away from civilization as it gets," Gerald agreed, "but I see no sign of any aborigine, or much of anything else for that matter." His not seeing, of course, didn't make it so. Riala, Leith, and Jane had once picnicked in the Murphy orchard where Riala had turned to an apparently empty landscape to ask the fruit and the trees if Noah would like to join in. It was only when Noah had said, "No thank you, missy," that Jane spotted him. What was so amazing was how Noah had been in plain view all the while.

Jane didn't doubt Noah was there now, if she could but coax him into revealing where.

"Come on, Noah! There's big trouble at The Facility. I want to make sure you don't go anywhere near there." Not that Noah would. He begrudged even his time spent in Keerborg and would have spent even less time there if he hadn't held out hope his son, Shem, would be influenced by Noah's sustained presence enough to take more interest in the old aborigine ways. Shem, though, was happier with white amenities. If Shem had inherited aspects of his father's diviner-ways—Shem had, after all, predicted the intensity of the present storm—there was little chance, as Jane saw it, that he would ever perfect them.

"Big trouble!" Noah agreed.

"Hey, do that again!" Evidently, Gerald thought Jane had thrown her voice with a ventriloquist's skill.

"We have to contact the authorities at Keerborg, Noah," Jane spoke to what appeared, for all purposes to Gerald and her, as a vacant landscape.

"Yes, please," Noah agreed.

"There!" Gerald finally spotted him.

Noah unfolded from a sparse patch of intertwined mulga and spinifex which seemed too insignificant to conceal even someone of his thin, diminutive size. "Very sharp eyes, mister," he congratulated.

"I'm sorry, Noah, that I screamed when I saw you in the car window," Jane apologized. "I was half asleep, and you weren't expected."

"*You* were expected," Noah surprised. "That is why I've come."

"How's that?" Gerald wanted to know.

Jane knew better than to ask, from past experiences. Noah had once told her exactly the time frame in which a certain rose would bloom in Riala's garden. How? Noah had shrugged when asked for specifics. Riala's explanation: she had shrugged, too.

"We have food and water, Noah," Jane thought to entice him closer; she should have known better.

"As do I," he replied. "The land provides."

Jane didn't doubt it, although she would have died on the spot had she any real need to make do with only what the sparse, stormy, desiccated surroundings provided.

"Can you tell us if the storm will give us more trouble, Noah?" she asked.

"More than one storm blows." He was cryptic as any Delphic oracle.

"Don't we know it," Gerald agreed.

"Can you tell us, though, if we're now safe?" she persisted.

"You and yours remain too much a mystery, and little good comes of it," Noah said.

"Amen to that," Gerald agreed. To Jane: "This beats fortune cookies."

"Have you come to talk of other things, then?" Noah must have wanted something, Jane reasoned, or he would never have materialized. She held no illusions that Gerald or she would have spotted him without his permission.

"I've something to give you," he said. "This something was thrown away, but its worth is different to different people." He pointed to their car. "Your machine is damaged but runs." It was a statement. "You will follow me with it, please."

Jane looked to Gerald for input.

"I wonder about the situation we've left at The Facility," Gerald said. "Would Noah be offended if we picked up whatever it is that he has for you later?"

"Remember the trouble I mentioned at The Facility, Noah," she tried. "It's very important we get to the authorities to tell them about it."

"What I have is between here and Keerborg." Noah turned and walked toward the still unseen town.

"And I had my heart set on hotcakes, eggs, ham, toast, jam, and coffee for a morning breakfast," Gerald fantasized. "I guess we'll have to settle yet again for trail bars."

Noah commenced a graceful, loping run; Gerald restarted the car in which Jane and he followed jerkily along after.

"I don't suppose he needs a ride?" Gerald mused. If Gerald could have run with such ease, he wouldn't have wanted to be in the car, either.

"I doubt he does." Jane had never seen Noah in a car, even in Keerborg.

An hour later, Gerald and Jane wiped the sweat from their faces as Noah maintained his graceful stride; the car chugged and groaned, creating a dust storm of its own.

"Where . . . ?" Gerald stopped the car with a screech.

"Don't ask me." Jane, too, had seen Noah one minute, and gone the next.

Car and occupants were caught in the rush of dust that had been following the vehicle. When the dust cleared, Jane got out. Gerald joined her.

Carefully, she checked the landscape. "Noah is just a man, and men don't disappear into thin air."

Gerald had his doubts. "Tell that to Noah."

She didn't see Noah, but she hadn't seen him, right off, earlier, either. Except, this time he'd asked them to follow, so why make it so difficult now? With still no sign of him, she swept the scene a second and a third time. "Over there!" she decided, pointing.

"Desert," Gerald identified all he saw. "More desert."

It took several long seconds before he finally spotted what she had: a small, dark A-shaped hole that angled almost imperceptibly downward into what appeared to be solid ground between the bases of two otherwise insignificant shoulder-high rocks.

"You're kidding!" he hoped.

"You've an alternative?"

"Noah does know we're humans, not moles, right?"

"He knows."

"But, he expects us to drop in—there?"

"So it would seem."

Walking the short distance together to the hole, they stopped just short of it. "It's dark in there, and it doesn't look any too big," Gerald said.

"They usually widen a little inside."

"'They?' Meaning, you've seen one of these

before?" He was dubious.

"I knew of one outside of Birdsville, when I was just a little girl."

"Dangerous place when it rains, yes?"

She laughed, because he had to have known his question was ridiculous. There were places in Australia where rain, perpetually nonexistent, never presented a problem.

The question, as she saw it, was, "Now what?"

"No chance Noah will reappear and give us the grand tour?"

"This hole probably doesn't look all that scary to him, remember?" she reminded. "It's just another home away from home. He probably never even figured we'd have trouble spotting it. Likewise, he probably never figured we'd have any qualms about letting ourselves in; white men in Australia certainly haven't stood on ceremony as far as most aborigine habitats."

"Any guess what's in there? Besides Noah, I mean."

William Maltese

"Not a clue," she admitted.

"Maybe we should mark this on the map and come back."

"Find it again, when we had such trouble this time?"

"You think it's important, then?"

"It's obviously important from Noah's standpoint," she qualified, "or he wouldn't have steered us here in the first place. Important to you? Important to me? Importance, like worth, is relative, especially when we've an appointment with the authorities in Keerborg to consider."

"An appointment that didn't exactly impress Noah."

She agreed. "One way or another, we're just wasting time, standing here."

"I'll not set foot in there without a light," he warned. Gerald went back to the car, and brought back a flashlight.

"If there are snakes around, we can be pretty

237

sure Noah's presence will have put them at a distance," Jane said, as if trying to convince herself.

"I'm just wondering if 'pretty sure' cuts the muster here." He bent low before the entranceway and entered through it in a low crouch. Just inside, he stopped and called ahead, "Any snakes, here we come!"

Jane followed.

At first, it definitely didn't look like much; she suspected it was meant to look that way. The floor was rough; the walls were flaky, dry soil; the ceiling was a matting of stalactite root systems that had extended deep for whatever moisture there was to be scavenged.

"Well, didn't you guess right that things would improve!" Gerald was more used to typical aborigine sites, like Kilbooling Cave, burrowed by man or nature in stone located well above ground.

"Old." She based her judgment on a preponderance of single-line petroglyphs suddenly appearing on walls now compacted and polished to red enamel.

"Trouble ahead!" He stopped and fanned the light.

"Just tell me it's not a snake."

"It's not a snake."

As it turned out, the branching of the tunnel wasn't a problem, in that Noah had specifically marked, with white stones placed in the shape of an arrow, the direction he intended them to go.

The gentle downward grade became steeper. The entrance diminished behind them to dime-size and then disappeared behind a curve of the passageway.

"Sometimes I wonder if the whole of Australia is honeycombed with an aborigine maze," he ventured, tempted to linger over a particularly fine segment of petroglyphs. On a second thought, he was becoming increasingly aware of the passing of time, the possible plight of their comrades, and wondered if they should stop and return to the surface.

Jane felt the guilt, too. "Maybe we *should* save this for another day."

He put his fingertips to his lips. They listened.

Jane thought she only imagined whatever it was she heard.

Gerald's "What's that?" was of marginal help.

The sounds returned: a distant sobbing and an eerie . . .

"Am I hearing your name being repeated over and over?" Gerald attempted decipherment.

Jane heard it, too, but she didn't believe it.

"Do you think Noah is playing a practical joke?" Gerald wasn't amused. "It isn't Halloween, is it?"

"Take it from me, Noah isn't a practical-joker," she assured.

The distant banshee wail continued, this time the soulful cry clearly stating, "Jane. Jane."

Jane got goose bumps that she doubted even a panacea hug from Gerald would cure. A good thing, too, since Gerald wasn't thinking of hugging her, combating instead gooseflesh of his own.

"Maybe if you answered?" he suggested. In his

240

mind, there was no doubt Jane was being summoned deeper into the depths. By Noah, whomever, or whatever was another thing all together.

"Hello!" Her attempt at an answer wasn't convincing. She had trouble getting it out; when she did, it waivered and cracked.

"Are you scared or something?" Gerald dropped his macho role: "If so, welcome to the club."

"Hello!" she tried again, this time with more determination

"Better," he congratulated. "It actually sounded like 'hello' that time."

The wailing stopped abruptly and was replaced by complete silence.

"So much for meaningful conversation, below ground, over great distance," she said and wondered again if they should turn back, or go forward. "I don't think we really should continue wasting our time like this," she offered.

"Right," he readily agreed.

This didn't, however, stop them from moving forward rather than back.

They paused only when they encountered what was obviously an underground room enlarged by human hands from the tunnel they were in. Gerald, sensing danger, held out a protective arm to keep her from squeezing by him.

He lit one side of the room with the flashlight beam and slowly panned it across the room towards the other side.

Animal skins were scattered on the floor and hung on the walls. An altar-like stone container overflowed with tubers, another with some kind of seed. Emu eggs, probably filled with water, glowed like fine porcelain on a makeshift table made less formidable by a tablecloth of soft-appearing animal skins in the dim spotlight.

When they heard the sound again, this time ear-piercingly loud, Gerald swung the flashlight to pinpoint the source of the anguish in the darkness.

"Oh!" Jane exclaimed when she identified, hard as it was, the genuine surprise the light revealed.

Dare to Love in Oz

Nine

"Diane?" Jane's voice was whispery with disbelief and uncertainty, since she thought she had to be mistaken. The "someone" on the kangaroo-fur rug was an emaciated shadow of the Diane Helms whom Jane remembered. This woman was dirty, gaunt, and wild-eyed, with hair tangled and matted.

"Noah!" Gerald's bellow shook dirt from the ceiling into a pebbly rain.

Jane went over to the poor creature on the rug, sat down beside her, and stared. Diane—yes, it was Diane—shied away. Had there been more room, she would have scuttled farther.

"We thought you were dead." Jane shifted some tangled hair from the woman's forehead.

"It's Jane and Gerald," Gerald identified and put Jane and his face alternatively within the beam of the flashlight. "From The Facility."

"Jane. Jane. Jane." Diane's chant was an eerie replay of the mantra that had drawn them to her in the labyrinth.

"Where's Noah?" Gerald's firm insinuation was that the aborigine was somehow tied to Diane's woe and was their only hope for valid information.

"His gift-giving done, I suspect he's vacated by another exit," Jane said. "I've a feeling he curses fate for his involvement, this far."

"Jane. Jane. Jane." Diane repeated soullessly.

"Yes, Diane. I'm here."

"Gerald?"

Gerald was pleasantly surprised. "Right on!"

Diane took Jane's hand and, with skeletal

fingers cracked and caked with dirt, held to it. She squeezed hard, as if milking the last juice from a green orange.

"He said you'd come . . . if I called. I didn't believe him," Diane said. "Then, when I heard you, I thought you were voices in my head, but you're real. Please! Please, be real!"

"We're real," Jane assured her.

"Certainly, we're real enough to question how you got here." Gerald hadn't expected Diane to be lucid, and he wanted to strike while the iron was hot. "This place is miles from Kronaol Ridge." As bad as Diane looked, she should have looked worse for having navigated the distance.

"Kronaol Ridge?"

"Sally left you there." Jane wondered if Diane's seemingly coherent comments, thus far, were merely disguising the confusion of the woman's mind.

"Sally left me at Golintoo Wash," Diane begged to differ.

"You must be . . ." Jane would have added "mistaken," but Gerald's hand on her arm stopped her.

"Left you?" he prodded.

Diane worked Jane's hand harder. "Sally said she'd left her lip balm in the car." Diane laughed, but there was no joy or amusement. "Then, she drove off and left me." Diane, what was still left of her, began sobbing uncontrollably, but there were no tears; her body had learned the hard way to conserve its moisture. "But why did she leave me?" Her eyes were wild with incomprehension.

Jane was perplexed. She didn't like Sally, never had, and to believe the worst was easy. Except, her dislike warned her to give Sally every benefit, lest she misjudge her.

Gerald was less reluctant to cast stones. "It would make certain things fit, wouldn't it, if we just allow our imaginations to try hard enough?"

Jane still had trouble with that. "What things?"

"Think about it." He figured Jane would see it,

too, given time. Trouble was, they were short on time, especially if Diane's tale of desertion were true. "What if Sally had expected more of the spotlight for the rare snake Ralph brought in, considering she'd helped him bag it? What if she was frustrated when all his research came to naught, the snake even dying in the bargain? What if Ralph moved on to something else, by way of research, to which Sally couldn't lay even partial claim? What if Sally was angry enough to kill Ralph, because he finally threw in the towel and eliminated any chance of any additional rub-off-on-her of his glory from their find?"

Jane thought those mighty big ifs. "You mean, all of this, and I do mean all of it, is Sally out to get back at Ralph, because he stymied her chances of jump-starting her flagging career?"

"What?" Diane obviously hadn't followed; Jane couldn't blame her.

"Everything is going to be fine, Diane." Jane's promise came easy. Reality would be something else again.

Jane turned to Gerald: "You think Sally poisoned herself? Gambled with something as dangerous as rust-snake poison?" Jane didn't buy his wild conjecture.

"Maybe she did, maybe she didn't." Gerald leaned toward believing the latter. "What about something less dangerous that gave similar symptoms? Anything to make her appear one of the gang until we'd all dropped dead. For that matter, she might have used the rust-snake toxin on herself, in order to pass later tests some specialist might give her, but she could have injected herself, too, with the antidote, even before you came along with the solution."

"Or, maybe she knew all along I'd have the answer," Jane divined, her own revelation staggering her imagination. "She knew I had natural immunity. I told her all about my snake bite at Tennant Creek back in the days when we were on chummier terms."

"Sally could easily have used that knowledge to

construct the perfect alibi." Gerald was now more convinced than ever. "Who would suspect her of anything when she appeared as much a potential victim as any of us? Your quick thinking to the rescue would have thrown one hell-of-a monkey wrench into the plan."

"Then, Ken *did* see Jake die in the car explosion!?" Jane said, feeling guilty as hell, if that were the case, in having beaned and, then, kept Ken a suspect to the end.

"Undoubtedly, Sally was improvising as the situation demanded," he decided, "but I'll bet what it all boiled down to, in the beginning, was her making Ralph's death appear accidental—the result of a completely unrelated lovers' triangle. Get rid of Diane; point the guilt at Ken or Jake. Jake and Ken killed in a car explosion; blame either one, it wouldn't matter which. Ken survives to attack us; accuse him. Jake's body isn't found; resurrect him as chief culprit. Steal Ralph's gun, fake an attack by it in the dark infirmary; convince us Ralph is somehow involved. Kill Ralph with poison; blame Jake,

blame Diane, blame anyone you bloody well please—
except Sally. She could have been using confusion to
mask her real goings-on."

"But why didn't Ralph respond to the antidote?"
Jane still blamed herself that she'd not been able to save
him.

"If Sally used anything other than rust-snake
poison on him, it would look suspicious at autopsy. In
fact, she wouldn't need another poison," he reasoned; he
felt he was on a roll. "Her intimate personal and
professional relationship with Ralph gave her every
opportunity to feed him increasing subclinical doses
over . . . say . . . three of four days—right up to the
moment she administered the lethal dose. He may have
looked or felt poorly, but none of us was up to par by
then."

"He said he thought he might be coming down
with some kind of bug. But if that was the effect of
prolonged poisoning, what kind of breakthrough could
Sally have expected that she would come so completely

252

unhinged and resort to murder when Ralph simply didn't provide it?"

"Anything that would put her back in the scientific limelight, even if it was only as second investigator, or, even, just as Ralph's assistant. You and I know she's become a bit of joke among her peers."

"Yes!" Diane interjected; Jane was surprised the woman had followed any of it; Jane's mind was still grasping. "Ralph had," Diane said hoarsely, "moved on to something new."

"However do you know that?" Gerald was no more sure than Jane that Diane was actually consciously part of the same conversation, but he wasn't about to pass over whatever she had just said.

"He'd finished with that non-toxin," Diane confirmed with finality.

"The non-toxin from the snake that bit Leith, you mean?" Jane thought it important to define parameters.

"I asked him about it over a late-night snack one

evening in the dining area," Diane said, gathering both strength and momentum as she spoke. "We'd both worked late; for once, Sally wasn't hanging around his neck like a clinging vine. I was as curious as everybody as to why he persisted in wasting his valuable time and genius on a non-toxin obviously going nowhere."

She stopped and looked suspiciously this way and that. Jane thought they'd lost her again to something other than pressing reality.

Gerald tried bringing her back. "Ralph said he had reached a dead-end with the non-toxin?"

"'Over and done!' that's what he told me," Diane said. "He was chucking the whole work and getting on to something more important. He'd only kept on for so long out of guilt over Leith's way of dying, hoping something could make the death meaningful: if cabbages were kings and horses could fly." Then, she said something that didn't fit: "He said you'd come."

"Ralph?" Jane's fingers were sore from Diane constantly kneading them.

"Noah." Diane had returned to the aborigine in her own round-about way. "He found me. I was dehydrated and sunburned. Near-dead from exposure. He carried me on his back, all of the way here. Running, would you believe, most of the way? He said I was to wait here for you, and you would come. Sure enough, here you are."

"And we're getting you out of here," Gerald promised, "right now."

"To where?" Jane's mind had already begun sorting alternatives. "To Keerborg?"

Gerald certainly saw Keerborg as one possibility, but the situation at The Facility, seen in this new light, might make continuing on to Keerborg less than the best course of action.

"Noah said I shouldn't go up top," Diane declined. "He said it was dangerous, and I was unfit to cope. I must make do down here: blankets, food, and water. I should wait, until . . ." She suddenly lost her train of thought.

"Until we got here," Jane completed for her. "And, we're here to take you out."

"Yes, please!" Diane sounded as pitiful as she looked. "It's so dark, I hate the dark." She released Jane, hugged herself, and hung her head listlessly.

Gerald gave her a hand. She was feather-weight; her skin felt to him like crinkly old parchment. The desert could do that, only too quickly, to those forced to face it unprepared. She had a lot to thank Noah for, not least of all for her life.

Either she looked far worse than she was, or she somehow mustered a reserve of strength, because she needed no assist to scuttle up and out of the hole, once assured she had permission to do so. She was noticeably wobbly upon exit, but, then, so was Jane who found the sudden return to wide open spaces and bright sunlight disorienting.

Once at the car, Gerald revealed what he'd been mulling over since just before they'd headed back up the tunnel. "We've lots more gas than we need to reach

Keerborg, but should that still be our prime objective?"

"The authorities are there." Jane saw it important to think this through.

"In order for them to be of use, they'll have to access The Facility," was Gerald's input. "Can that happen any time soon?"

Automatically, Jane looked to the horizon beyond which The Facility existed. That sky and landscape were still rife with red dust. No matter that it was clear and windless directly above. That Cole got his helicopter down at The Facility wasn't likely to be duplicated by any additional helicopters flown in from Keerborg, at least not while there was still so much dust and wind enwrapping the installation.

"A half a day's more drive to Keerborg," Gerald reminded, "and a day to drive back if there's no getting in with the choppers. What happens to unsuspecting Cole and Peter in the meantime?"

"You think Sally will kill them?" Jane shuddered.

He wasn't encouraging. "Another death or two would simply add further to the confusion, yes?"

"Surely, though, she wouldn't . . ." Jane brought herself up short. All it took was a look at Diane, burrowing like a frightened rabbit into one corner of the car, to know that anyone who had left a person in the desert without food or water was capable of anything.

Gerald cast his vote, "I say we go back. Make some excuse for our return. Say the storm was impossible to get through. Say the car broke down. Sally needn't know we're onto her and back to lock her up first chance we get."

"You don't think she'll be clued in by Diane's resurrection?" Jane knew otherwise.

He pursed his lips. "What if we leave Diane, the supplies, and the car at Kilbooling Cave?"

"And what if we don't get back to her?" Jane was determined that they consider all possibilities.

"There'll still be enough fuel for her to make the drive to Keerborg on her own."

"Barring unforeseen obstacles, and if she can drive," Jane felt obliged to remind.

"Can you drive, Diane?" he queried.

Diane curled even tighter into her corner of the backseat.

"I'd just like to do everything we can, as quickly as we can, for Peter and Cole," Gerald admitted.

"And if Peter and Cole are already dead?" Jane played the devil's advocate. "Granted, Sally may want a couple of survivors to verify how she was as much a victim as anyone else, allowing that there's bound to be some kind of investigation and questions. But, couldn't she just as well figure you and I are witnesses enough? She can't know we'd run into a live and kicking Diane on our way to Keerborg."

"Go back to The Facility!" Diane surprised them, although she didn't go so far as to come uncurled. "Sally will kill them. She's crazy as a Mad Hatter! As for me, if I survived the desert and that aborigine hole in the ground, I can survive Kilbooling Cave and any eventual drive to Keerborg."

That resolved, they headed back toward The Facility and, worst, into the storm that still refused to let the institution free of its clutches.

"You'd think, by now, this thing would have blown itself out," Jane complained, undeniably depressed to be back inside it. "Or, shouldn't it at least be halfway across the continent by now?"

Diane again proved she wasn't completely out of it by summoning up a bit of thoroughly unappreciated trivia, "One such storm settled in over Milparinka in the twenties and stayed two months."

As the car backtracked, Jane was made increasingly ill-at-ease by the absence of any additional surprises. When they managed to get as far as Kilbooling Cave, without any incident, she was genuinely paranoid. Oh, the storm blew the car, and it blew dust everywhere, into every nook and cranny of the vehicle and their clothed bodies; it engulfed them in zero visibility on occasion; it made breathing a constant chore of separating sufficient oxygen from the overabundant grit; but, all of that was par for the course. Where was the assault by lightning, the attack by a killer tree, and the death-trap sand dune barricading the roadway?

If she expected to be doubly assaulted by the elements during yet another on-foot crossing of the terrain between the cave and The Facility, she was deprived even of that by Diane's sensible suggestion: "I'll drive you to within easier walking distance." This from a woman Jane had assumed, just a few hours before, to be pretty much dead. Nor had Diane appeared all that revived, despite her bouts of lucid conversation, during which Gerald and Jane had provided her in short, tolerable installments all the macabre details, including the deaths of Diane's husband and Ken.

"You're sure you want to drive us?" Gerald sounded as doubtful as Jane felt about Diane's condition.

"You want a ride or not?" Diane wasn't up to a debate. She'd need all of her strength and concentration to get them to The Facility and get herself back to the cave. This didn't mean she didn't feel up to the task. She already realized that Noah had done especially well by her. Next time she met up with him, she determined she would do something to repay her debt to him.

She came out of her momentary reverie to see Jane and Gerald still looking doubtfully at her.

"If you want to walk, I'm quite prepared to wave you good-bye without further protest," she said. "Just remember that someone in my line of business, doing research out in this hell-hole, in the first place, doesn't have the characteristics of a delicate, hot-house flower. I've survived, thus far, and I have every intention of surviving well beyond my stay in this cave and beyond whatever is required to get you a few yards closer to The Facility in relative safety."

Admittedly, neither Gerald nor Jane really wanted to repeat the walk that had been far from pleasurable their first time through. Both reluctantly consented, even with Gerald raising the further specter of their being seen.

Once underway, their heretofore nemesis, the wind, obliged by concealing their car's approach as far as the southernmost edge of The Facility's sand-scoured, glass-gabled still. Even so, Gerald and Jane felt genuinely certain there would be something to pay for any accommodation now.

Diane dropped them off before the storm could change its mind about letting her deliver them and, also, let her return to the cave under its cloak of protection.

As soon as Diane and the car were gone, Gerald pulled Jane into the lee of one of the glass gables and kissed her to remind him of the sweetness of her lips mingled with the powder of desert dust.

Jane slipped a hand into his, and together they loped half-bent over to the dome. A glimpse of possible movement off to one side made her fears, that none of this was destined to run smoothly, come rushing back.

Gerald recognized her skittishness immediately.

"Don't look now," she said, trying for calm, cool, and collected, "but the camera to our right is following us."

There were cameras positioned all around the grounds, but what made this one special was that it appeared undusted and operational.

"Peter must have fixed it," Gerald suggested.

Jane saw no reason for optimism. "If it sees us, it likely saw the car drop us off, and Diane behind the wheel."

"Maybe the lens is too scoured," he suggested. "Maybe there's no one monitoring the screen."

"Peter would recognize Diane. He'd spread the 'good' word to Sally who'd recognize it as anything but good news for her."

"Cole, Peter, and Sally are three people with plenty of things to do and places to be, besides hanging out together in the security cubicle, checking out activity in this particular sector of the compound at this moment."

Jane tried to be as positive, "Why should Sally get all the breaks? Is that what you're really saying?"

They accessed the dome's interior by using

Jane's I.D.; at least Sally hadn't canceled that. It didn't escape Jane, though, that a second camera on the front gate also seemed functional.

Once inside, Jane made sure no one was behind the reception-room mosaic, where Ralph had once lurked and surprised her.

The door to the stairs opened with a startling bang. Gerald and Jane automatically swung loaded pistols at the form of Cole who stumbled out and collapsed to both knees, hands to head, and bellowed, "Bloody pain!"

Gerald moved first. Jane stayed put to cover the door with her gun. Gerald grabbed Cole by the collar and bodily pulled the man out of the open and into comparative cover off to one side. Jane then joined them.

"Now if we can just isolate Peter," Jane said and wondered the odds of achieving that.

"No!" Cole grabbed Jane's sleeve.

Gerald and Jane exchanged glances.

Cole managed to brace himself in a sitting position against the wall. "Please, my headache is more bearable when I don't move."

Jane registered no surprise that his head still hurt, even though his x-rays had turned up absolutely nothing; the skull and the gelatinous brain it protected were often elusive with their secrets—medical or otherwise.

"Peter's gone," Cole gasped. "Sally told him she'd heard noises. He and she went to investigate. They split up to search. He vanished without a trace. She said she hadn't a clue where."

"What about Sally?" Jane didn't want to dwell on the possibilities of Peter lured somewhere and disposed of by Sally.

"You tell me! She tried to kill me, didn't she?" Cole shook his head. "Can you believe it?"

Oh, yes! Jane was a true believer.

"Just minutes ago, in the security cubicle," Cole elucidated. He pushed himself into an almost standing position, winced, shut his eyes, and seemed to wait for the pain to ease. "Peter fixed several cameras before he dropped out of sight. Sally and I were checking the monitors for signs of Peter or Jake."

Poor, dumped-on dead-in-the-car-explosion Jake! Jane thought.

"We spotted your car pulling up outside," Cole continued. "You got out. Someone stayed in the car. Sally said it was someone called Diane." Cole arched an eyebrow. "Who's Diane?"

"We've lots to tell you," Jane assured, then emphasized, "but only when you're finished telling us everything."

"Sally pulled a gun, turned it on me, and fired. What else is there to tell? I haven't a clue why the bullet didn't hit me. I must have moved too fast, or she must have been more anxious to leave than stick around to finish me off. What's it all about?"

They told him.

"So Sally blew my chopper?" Cole's amazement was obvious.

"Sally did it all," Gerald summated. "Diane's

return from the dead meant there were soon going to be questions Sally wasn't prepared to answer. It sounds as if she panicked."

"Amazing!" Cole said. He started to shake his head but apparently thought better of it.

"If Sally's killed Peter . . ." Jane didn't even want to think about it.

Gerald took the stairs two at a time to the infirmary to check it out. Arriving uneventfully, he signaled that it was okay for Jane and Cole to follow.

Once ensconced, the three figured there was more safety in numbers and decided to stay put. If they just waited out the storm, they could count upon people finally beginning to question why there were no open lines of communication remaining between The Facility and the outside world. While they were at it, they could just as realistically hope for a hot pizza-with-everything-on it delivered to the front door.

Cole volunteered to take the first watch. "Better let me do my duty while I'm feeling up to it. I'm never sure when the pain will return. Luckily, so far, it comes on gradually with forewarning, so I can wake one of you up if it gets too bad."

Jane and Gerald agreed and snuggled up together in a corner, guns on laps, ready to awaken on instant notice. Jane dreamed of Sally and heard the woman say, "Looks as if I won't have to wake her after all!"

Jane opened her eyes to find the nightmare continuing: "Surprise!" Sally had a gun and was pointing it directly at Jane. "So you decided to join the party?"

Jane blinked, making an attempt to summon a better reality. She saw Gerald awake, sitting nearby, looking very angry.

Sally followed Jane's glance in Gerald's direction and laughed at what she saw. "Jane is confused, Gerald. What a relief to know even her genius, at times, can be circumvented."

Cole stood near Sally and slightly behind her. Jane figured he could, if very fast, grab Sally and disarm her. Instead, Cole said calmly, "Why don't you let me take the gun for awhile, Sally?"

Jane groaned. Only in a dream would Cole think it rational to calmly ask so insane a woman as Sally to surrender her weapon.

Only in a dream would so insane a woman as Sally smile so sweetly and turn her gun over to him.

Only in a dream would Cole turn the gun on the still smiling Sally and pull the trigger.

Ten

Unfortunately, it was no dream!

Jane recognized the grim reality with the ear-splitting explosion of the gun, the dull splat of the bullet, the rapid blossom of blood, and the surprised expression on Sally's face as the bullet lodged within her and propelled her violently against the wall.

The bizarreness of the event made Jane feel terrified, and she had every right to be.

"You two stay put!" Cole warned. Although he'd shot Sally, he kept Gerald and Jane carefully within his peripheral vision.

"What . . . ?" Jane was genuinely speechless.

"Cole was in it with Sally, all along," Gerald filled Jane in on one part of the puzzle that was escaping her.

"Cole? Sally?" Jane was dumb-founded. How could she have come awake to this?

"The two worked together to kill Peter soon after we were gone." Gerald didn't know for sure, but that's how he suddenly had it figured.

"No!" Jane refused to believe Peter was dead.

"Afraid so," Cole admitted with a shrug.

Jane shivered all of the way to her toes. "But why?" No getting around it, she was stunned by Cole's betrayal.

"Do I really want to take the time to enlighten you?" In apparent afterthought, Cole used the still-smoking barrel of his gun to scratch his forehead. It seemed an open invitation for Jane, or Gerald, or both to rush him, so he could kill one or both of them and not bother with time-consuming explanations. "I hate to see real life mimicking pulp fiction and B-movies, but there is a decided temptation to put it all on the table, unravel the weave, so to speak, so at least two threads, if even for just a moment, can appreciate the complexity woven by real genius."

Jane repressed an urge to tell him just what she thought of his genius, a.k.a. treachery, but, whatever the outcome, she wanted answers; bad-mouthing him wouldn't get them for her.

"Then again," he continued when neither Jane nor Gerald gave him the expected response, "if I get bored in the telling, I can cut it off any time, can't I?"

"How did you, Cole Wilcott, ever get involved with the likes of Sally Falwen?" Jane continued to blame Sally for the whole mess.

"In point of fact, Cole Wilcott didn't." His smile was rife with self-satisfaction. There was no doubt he thoroughly enjoyed the confusion he was causing with that ambiguous revelation. "Jurgen Blenge is the name. Never had the privilege of meeting the real Cole Wilcott."

Jane knew what she'd just heard, but believing it was something else. "You're not Cole Wilcott?"

When Jurgen finally spoke again, it was as if he addressed a far larger audience: "Originally, the plan was for me literally to fly by, the convenient storm allowing me the excuse of being downed by bad weather. The idea of my taking on Cole Wilcott's identity came from Sally radioing me before she trashed The Facility communications system. You, Jane, had called in to report that you were meeting Cole, for the very first time, and he was flying you in from Keerborg. Sally had ferreted out those personal and useful tidbits, as well as how Cole was suddenly downed by the storm at Grenpewrie Station and never got to Keerborg. That left me the opportunity to play him and to intercept you, Jane, at Keerborg. You, though, had driven off to rendezvous with Gerald to run the storm all of the way back here.

"How convenient and absent of suspicion it would have been for me to have arrived here with Jane, she introducing me all around as Cole. As it worked out, though, it wasn't all that bad. Of course, there was always the outside chance that someone here might know what the real Cole looked like, but it seemed unlikely; he's not exactly made himself readily available to the press lately, and the outback has been known to change overnight the looks of people subjected to its rigors. Cole and my hair colors are basically one and the same, and I was careful to comb my hair into his style I remember from an early photo when he first arrived in Australia. Extremely beneficial was how toxicologists and ex-greengrocers-turned-opal-prospectors don't normally travel within the same social circles, scientists well-known for the professionally inbred lives they lead, and Cole long having had the reputation of let-me-live-my-life-in-peace, shying away from publicity and press.

"Anyway, I *became* Cole, and I flew into Keerborg to ferry Jane here. However, some young aborigine, who worked for Riala Murphy, said Riala had driven Jane to meet you, Gerald, and the two of you would be driving here. I followed along and, knowing the situation that had developed here, since I'd played a major part in planning it, I was able to bide my time and choose just the right moment and way to miraculously appear."

"You're mad!" Jane's fury, of course, was equally aimed at herself for having been duped.

"You won't get away with this!" Gerald insisted. The problem was that he couldn't, at the moment, see why not.

Jurgen's smile revealed just how much weight he gave either's opinion. "Shall I tell you how one very blown-up helicopter, just outside these perimeters, will further muddy the water? Will you really appreciate the subtle shading offered by that chopper having been rented under the name of Jeremy Darunge, a man who once threatened Peter Sils over a slut in a Darwin bar?" He laughed, and it wasn't a pleasant sound for either Jane or Gerald to hear. "In fact—" He winked at Jane. "—my man who rented the chopper looks very much like Jeremy Darunge. The real Jeremy, this very minute, is somewhere with a very attractive woman, in a very secluded love nest, and will soon be unable to provide any valid alibi for his time spent while all the chicanery was happening out here."

"Such a complicated woof you weave, in order to deceive," Gerald had to admit, "but to what possible purpose?"

"Never did have that figured out, did you?" Jurgen said and shook his head. His fabricated headaches had evaporated when he eliminated Sally and shed his Cole Wilcott persona.

"I know I never figured it out," Jane admitted. Nor was she willing to go to her untimely death not knowing.

"The secret was well kept because Ralph was so secretive," Jurgen allowed them. "Poor Ralph. He would have preferred that not even Sally knew, but Sally was so determined to wheedle her way into claiming whatever bit of notoriety resulted from the discovery of that new-to-the-scientific-world snake that she was into his private notes as often as she was into his bed."

"You're talking about whatever new project Ralph began to work on after he decided that the non-toxic snake research was getting him nowhere?" Jane prodded. She was closer, but she still didn't have the answers she so desperately wanted.

"What new project?" Jurgen asked with a tone that suggested to Jane that even he might not happen to know everything of this labyrinthine serial.

"Diane told us that Ralph had begun a new research project," she said, determined to keep Jurgen talking.

"Ah, Diane," he said, "the dear lady who Sally decided not to kill outright, as instructed, but to leave to the wiles of the Australian outback? Whose return from the wilderness it was only sheer luck that Sally and I witnessed as Diane delivered you on our doorstep and drove off again? It was also pure luck for us that Peter had gotten around to repairing that portion of the viewer security system before it became imperative for us to remove him from the equation. Ah, what interesting aspects might have been provided had Diane managed to arrive and disappear without being spotted? Not that things would have turned out any differently, mind you, since Diane would hardly have been able to point any kind of accusing finger in my direction, and I would have been there when you grabbed poor unawares Sally. Speaking of dear Diane, you two do know that I'm going to have to pay her a visit at Kilbooling Cave before I completely vacate the area, don't you? You did say that's where she's waiting, didn't you?"

Jane genuinely felt badly for Diane, having brought that woman back from one danger to an even greater one than Diane had faced in the outback, but, right now, Jane's main concern was far more selfishly motivated. "You still haven't gotten around to your motive."

He pursed his lips, as if in thought. He was playing the cat with two mice and apparently enjoying it. Jane knew it but didn't care, as long as he got around—

eventually—to telling her what she wanted to know. The longer they could keep him talking . . . "Motive?" she repeated.

"If Ralph ever told Diane that he had ceased research on the snake," he said, "and I don't, for a minute, question that he did, I can tell you that it would have been a lie. He was, you see, genuinely frightened that someone might learn what he had finally learned; namely, the snake serum in question was toxic after all."

"Leith's autopsy left no doubt but that he died of heart malfunction due to a congenital heart defect," Jane reminded. "No trace whatsoever of toxicity from the snake bite."

"All true," he gave her that much.

She waited, and he made her wait.

Gerald broke before either of them did. "Why don't you spell it out for us?"

Simultaneously, Gerald and Jane had a sudden inkling of what all of this might mean, and the possibilities it offered to the likes of Jurgen. The revelation made them queasy.

"I suppose you two know that I'm doing just what I've always told myself I'd never do," Jurgen said with a slight roll of his eyes which in no way diverted his attention from them. "After such confessions in movies and books, don't the heroine and hero always turn the tables on the villain? It isn't likely, however, that you'll turn the tables on me, unless, of course, I do something exceedingly stupid to give you the advantage. Which you have less chance of seeing happen than a snowball has of seeing a long life in hell."

"Let me make an educated guess," Jane suggested. "The snake poison from that snake is so slow-working that Leith's congenital heart defect simply and quite unrelatedly beat it to the punch."

"Good start, but do go on."

"Go on?" She wasn't at all sure where to take it from there.

"Ah, but Ralph's discovery is so much more deliciously exciting than that," he chided. "Surely, you haven't forgotten all of those mysteriously dead rats, all having originated in Ralph's lab cubicle."

"All dead of snake toxin!" Gerald didn't make it a question. The queasiness resulting in the pit of his belly, put there by his increasing suspicions that Jurgen might well live to benefit from all of this mayhem and murder, brought up bitter bile that Gerald tasted in his throat.

"Was that Jane and your combined verdict when you examined them?" Jurgen asked.

"We didn't conduct nearly enough experiments to pin down cause," Jane remembered.

"Oh, further experimentation would have netted you no different short-term results," Jurgen waved aside her protests. "Believe me when I tell you that Ralph conducted all the tests there are to give and finally had to devise his own to pin down the nasty reality."

"Please, don't tell me you are an international assassin, or work for some nefarious government." Gerald's uneasiness had turned to quiet panic.

"Please don't tell me that either one of you is so

naive as to think that all governments, nefarious or otherwise, won't be right in there, bidding enthusiastically, when they know what I'm going to put on the auction block," Jurgen countered. "After all, we're talking venom that's colorless, odorless, tasteless, and easily absorbed through the skin; meaning, no need for injection, or ingestion, *and* it's uniformly fatal, inducing death sufficiently after exposure as to make any association difficult. Add to that, it does its work without leaving any tracer known to the scientific world at large. Think of its potential in assassinations; or, when synthetically mass-produced, consider its potential for chemical welfare. Spray an enemy with it today, and who's going to blame you for deaths that begin happening weeks, even months later, or, with some minor chemical variations well within the grasp of most such groups, maybe even years from now?"

"I can't believe even Sally would stoop so low," Jane said, except that she really could believe it. Now that she knew what was at stake, she had to stall for time.

Either she, or—please, please—Gerald had to formulate some kind of a plan not only to get free but to stop Jurgen from introducing such potential for undetected disasters into the world.

"You and your peers really should have been far nicer to poor Sally," Jurgen offered with a cluck-cluck of his tongue against the roof of his mouth. "She knew you all looked upon her pretty much as a joke. It was to prove herself to the likes of you that she jumped at the chance to help Ralph capture that unique snake. All Sally wanted was a bit of limelight. She had, of course, had some past successes, mostly at the beginning of her career, just enough to get a taste for fame before realizing that it had all been more luck than any real talent on her part. Ralph, on the other hand, wasn't mediocre. He was a real genius, in fact. All by himself, he came up with the discovery that could have made Sally and him bywords within certain select, and very influential, government circles. Imagine poor Sally's chagrin when Ralph made it clear to her that he had no intentions of sharing it with her. To whom else could Sally turn, in her moment of need, than to someone who could give her not only a plan of action but the promise of enough money to let her find a new and active life among the independently *nouveau riche*? She knew I could be generous, in that I'd already been using her for years as a mole to keep an eye on any of her associates' breakthroughs that I might be able to tap for financial gain before the competition could move in. No denying that she hit the jackpot, albeit quite accidently, this time around. Too bad she wasn't able to stick around long enough to enjoy it."

He didn't look or sound in the least bit sorry.

"All the murders committed for a poison." Gerald didn't make it a question. It sounded fantastic, but he knew with dead certainty that it was true.

"Chaos," Jurgen said. "Red-herrings, as the mystery writers like to say. Diversions. Confusions. Scapegoats. Mazes within labyrinths within puzzles, *ad infinitum*. And, when I leave here, I shall ransack the whole place, scatter all its papers, detach labels, and smash vials. In the end, no one will be able to tell what's missing, even if they had more to go on, which I assure you they won't. The police will end up chasing their proverbial tails, while I'm away with the prize, free and clear. Maybe a bit messier than I would have hoped, but Ralph was on the verge of destroying his notes, as well as the remaining venom, and I was forced to move quickly. In the end, I suspect, far more people will end up dead than just those who perished hereabouts because of my hurried improvisations, all of course based upon Sally's invaluable input about on-site romances and whatever."

He walked over to one side of the room and retrieved a briefcase. He opened the case's lid. Inside were a small, hardback notebook and one sealed, partially full vial of clear liquid. The latter was cushioned within a plastic ice pack.

He tipped the case so that Jane and Gerald were sure to see. "Have you any real conception of just what these are worth on the open market?"

"Whatever their worth, it's not nearly enough to

compensate for the horrors committed to get them," Jane assured him.

He snapped the case shut; Jane knew they'd stretched his confession about as far as he was prepared to allow them. He showed no intentions of lowering his guard to allow Jane or Gerald to make anything other than a suicidal move to extract them from a situation growing ever more precarious.

Rescue came from a source so unexpected that Jane and Gerald, as surprised as Jurgen by the turn of events, found themselves momentarily glued to the spot and struck dumb, even after the presumed-dead Sally had risen from the floor, barreling at Jurgen with a loud and eerie scream, "You bastard!"

The sound of the gunshot said Jurgen had recovered sufficiently to switch his aim from Gerald and Jane to his attacker and to fire. But where his first shot had blasted Sally back against the wall, this later one, after thudding into her, barely countered Sally's forward momentum, slowing but not stopping her. She collided solidly with Jurgen with a crunch … arms flaying and fingernails clawing to inflict maximum hurt.

Jurgen went backward and down from the impact of their collision. Had he lost his gun, at that moment, it might have given Jane the necessary impetus for further offensive action. As it was, she watched dumbly fascinated, like a doe caught in the glare of a spotlight, as the deadly drama unfolded in seeming slow motion before her.

It was Gerald who dashed forward to snatch up the momentarily ignored briefcase, even as Jurgen was again pulling the trigger of his weapon to put yet another bullet into Sally who'd fallen atop him.

Jane reached for Gerald's free hand at the same moment he reached out for her; the two, with briefcase, headed for the door. A bullet from Jurgen's gun followed them and chewed a large piece of plaster from the nearby wall.

Gerald and Jane took to the stairs at top speed, intuitively knowing where they were headed; no jerky this-way that-way pulling against one another to impede their flight this time.

In the garage, Gerald released her hand, slammed the fire door shut behind them, and flattened himself against the shut barricade. Jane suspected the door was thick enough to prevent the penetration of a bullet from the other side, but her scientific mind wasn't up to the necessary computations of bullet mass and velocity as opposed to door composition and density to be sure. "We need to block the door with sometimes besides handsome you!" she ended up insisting; no way was she taking any more chances like moments ago.

"Back up one of the cars, then," Gerald told her. Jane hadn't forgotten the cars were initially and probably remained booby-trapped with explosives, but neither had Gerald. "Peter said the bombs were set to go off after the cars put on some mileage. The distance from that car—" He nodded toward the nearest vehicle. "—and this door is only a matter of feet."

They knew, of course, that Peter might have

been mistaken. That Jurgen had admitted to being on an accelerated schedule, though, due to Ralph's decision to destroy his notes and the venom, implied there would have been insufficient time to wire each car with a different type of bomb.

Nonetheless, her hands sweated profusely as she grabbed a key from the metal key box and ran for the car in the corresponding parking space. Just in case, she shut her eyes when she turned the ignition; made a gasping little sound when she engaged the reverse gear; and came very near hyperventilating by the time the car was actually on the move.

Gerald stepped out of the way as the rear fender of the vehicle Jane drove collided with a resounding crunch against the very spot on the door in front of which Gerald's knees had been located seconds before.

Jane was painfully aware that she had used far more acceleration than intended. She shuddered at the possibility of how the resulting minor collision not only might have injured Gerald but might as well have jogged the explosive mechanism and prematurely set off the bomb. Awash in the undeniable truth that Gerald and she were still alive, she released her iron grip on the steering wheel and would likely have flowed, like melted butter, down the seat and onto the floor, if there hadn't been far more vital matters to consider.

"You okay?" Gerald opened the door on the driver's side, without Jane even knowing, to be there for her.

"I don't have my gun," was all she could think to say. It was a delayed response, in that she had been unarmed since she'd awoke to the unexpected apparition of Sally in the infirmary.

"Jurgen confiscated both our weapons while we were asleep." Gerald told her what she already knew.

"We have to get to Diane at Kilbooling Cave," Jane decided. If they didn't want to walk, they'd have to defuse at least one of the remaining car bombs. Defusing the car that was now with Diane at the cave had been a daunting task even for Peter who had undertaken it only with professional reservations and accomplished it with difficulty.

Gerald couldn't imagine himself a qualified member of any bomb squad. "I'm afraid my knowledge of explosives is at a dangerous minimum," he felt compelled to admit.

"If we can't use the cars, then we can at least take all the car keys with us so Jurgen can't defuse and use a car to catch up to us," Jane said. There was no way to know Jurgen's expertise with cars or car bombs, but it was safe to assume he had knowledge at least comparable to, if not superior to, Sally who had likely installed the devices.

"For double protection, we can take and smash the distributors," Gerald added. "Maybe we can get him to waste valuable time trying to hot-wire the cars before he checks under the hood."

Gerald further suggested, then rejected, that they search for a car jack to lift the back of one car, start its motor, put it in gear, and jam down its gas pedal with something, letting the rear wheels spin the miles until detonation. The Facility had been designed to withstand major natural catastrophes. Even a high-magnitude earthquake was supposed to leave it not only standing but fully operational. However, who knew how badly its structural integrity would be compromised by a quick series of explosions of unknown combined intensity, set off, nearly simultaneously, within the garage? Maybe the thick walls would sufficiently contain the blasts. Maybe the force of the explosions would blow down the outside door; maybe it would dislodge the fire door Gerald and Jane had barricaded, and take care of anyone who happened to be standing behind it.

Then again, what if the force of the explosions compromised the poison storage area and released all of the deadly stored toxins, maybe even vaporizing some in the process? The imagined consequences held the potential for an unmitigated environmental disaster and squelched any chances of Jane and Gerald making it happen.

"Leave two cars capable of running," Gerald brought Jane out of the dark reverie into which she had fallen while opening one car hood after another to remove distributor caps.

"I'm sorry?" She thought she'd misheard.

"No denying the advantage of a head start," he reminded, "and if each of us drives a car out of here, we can, when safely away, weigh down accelerator pedals and send the vehicles off in opposite directions as decoys. Jurgen can't know if we've decided to bypass Diane and Kilbooling Cave in a higher priority move to get that—" He nodded toward the rescued briefcase. "—out of his mad, money-grubbing clenches; nor will he know for certain when the cars explode, if we were in one or both of them."

Jane wasn't taken with the idea of their trying to drive two time bombs away from The Facility. What if the bombs went off sooner than expected? What if only one bomb went off? What if . . .?

"Jane?" Gerald guessed from her stare that her

thoughts were wandering, and he needed her focused and with him, here and now.

"I'm fine," she insisted; *not true*, she thought, *but where was the harm in a bit of positive thinking*!?

They recovered a tool box from the trunk of each of the two cars they left operational and transferred each tool box to the front seat of its respective vehicle. The boxes should provide adequate weight to assure that the gas pedals remained solidly depressed, when the time arrived.

"I'll go first," he said. "You follow in the second car with the briefcase."

Gerald's thinking went like this: Jurgen hadn't appeared as they feared and expected at the fire door. That meant he'd had plenty of time to head outside and take up a spot from which to ambush them. The first car to leave would be the more vulnerable.

"We'll flip a coin for lead-off position," she insisted.

"Jane, this is hardly the . . ."

"We'll flip a coin," she interrupted firmly. "It's not a subject up for debate. Heads, you get the lead; tails . . ."

She flipped a coin she had been carrying in her pocket, caught it, and showed him the tails-side up on the back of her left hand. She appreciated how he accepted, albeit hardly without a frown, the reality that they were going to be equals in this to the bitter end. To Jane's way of thinking, Gerald was not to be burdened with a mantle of leadership simply because of the accident of his sex at birth.

Starting the two remaining operable cars at the same time was a doubly tense moment. As Jane drove her car forward to assume lead position, she imagined she could hear the bomb in her car ticking; a cursory search, however, showed that the ticking issued from the dashboard clock.

She activated the garage door remote control and watched the massive door begin its excruciatingly slow unveiling of the dangerous world awaiting them on the outside.

Dare to Love in Oz

Eleven

The sunlight surprised Jane; firstly, as it spread quickly into the garage; secondly, as its glare engulfed her. Without hesitation, she sped directly into it.

She had just raised a hand to shade her eyes from the overwhelming glare when her windscreen spit and splintered into a sunburst of fissures around what could be nothing less than a bullet hole.

She swerved the car reflexively and hit the still-unseen Jurgen, tossing him over the hood only to have his face smash against the windscreen. The cracked glass caved in towards her.

She screamed and slammed the brakes. The car stopped abruptly, throwing Jurgen forward into the sunshine, like a rock from a sling.

Jane locked the car doors; an effort, she knew, that would be worthless if Jurgen still had his gun and was able to use it.

Sunlight, magnified and refracted into splashes of blazing colors by the fractured windscreen, made it impossible for Jane to see much. The best she could do in the situation was to drive the driveway as she remembered it. It turned out to be the right decision, because the glare reduced once she headed back under a sky still pocketed by dust clouds. By scooting down in the seat, she could actually see through the last of the undamaged front-window glass.

A side mirror reflected Gerald's car in close proximity, as well as Jurgen, farther back, the latter getting up off the side of the road. Jane didn't know how badly Jurgen was injured, nor did she care. All that was important was putting as much distance as Gerald and she could between them and the madman.

Of all the times the storm might have chosen to blow its last, it had waited until Jane would have preferred it renew its previous fury to mask their exit from The Facility. However, the storm's failure to cooperate was just another of the many obstacles she was totally determined to overcome.

She stopped the car; Jurgen menaced from a distance. Jane imagined him running for her, gun aimed to accomplish through the back car window what he had unsuccessfully accomplished through the front. Yanking the remote control unit off the dashboard, she reciprocated, aiming it back towards him and The Facility. She wished it were a gun to blast him away where he stood, but she settled for the familiar slow closing of the garage door behind him.

If she expected him to shift his attention and make a last chance run to access The Facility, she was disappointed: He stayed put; although once the door completely closed, he would have to waste valuable time going around and somehow breaking down the barrier Jane and Gerald had erected when they lodged a parked car against the inside of the garage's fire door.

Gerald gave a loud beep of his car horn to encourage Jane to leave the stranded Jurgen to whatever his fate and, at the same time, draw Jurgen's attention away from the closing door. No more anxious than Gerald to linger, Jane ground her car back into gear and accelerated down the road.

She checked the odometer and tried to determine where she'd find the wreckage of the car that had exploded poor Jake to Kingdom Come. No sign of it; still, she suspected it couldn't be far off.

Another attention-getting beep from Gerald's car horn informed her that he was no more willing than she to await definite signs of the wreckage to determine how far they could safely drive their rolling time bombs from The Facility.

Jane stopped her car and watched as Gerald exited his and hiked the distance to her window which she rolled down. There was no sign of Jurgen in the distance.

"Pull up another twelve yards," he instructed and leaned against the open window ledge so that his handsome face was within kissing distance, "to where that bed of hard rock is exposed."

Jane's first inclination was to ask, *What bed of hard rock?* She'd been this way before and thought she had its topography down by heart; in afterthought, she knew better. The storm would have shifted millions of tons of sand. Where once there had been bulldozer loads of granulated mineral crystals, there might now be an area swept clean down to the hard, blue-black bedrock characteristic of the area.

"If Jurgen gets this far, it'll be harder for him to spot our footprints on stone to tell him we exited both cars," Gerald clarified.

Jane reluctantly drove her car ahead as instructed and aimed it off on a tangent to what was left of the old roadway that she'd followed thus far. She stopped the car and opened the tool box in the adjoining front seat to retrieve the jump cables with which she laced and secured the steering wheel to assure the car would continue forward, when left on its own, and not circle or be turned by its first encounter with a rut or rock. Then, with some difficulty, she propped the again-closed tool box, one end to the floor at her feet, the other end poked above the edge of the seat between her legs. She put the car into first gear and, with some very deft maneuvering, managed to slip the tool box onto the gas pedal. She quickly exited the car as it began its slow driverless ride across the black bedrock and into the sandy wilderness that stretched from horizon to horizon.

By the time Jane exited, Gerald, too, had set his car off on its own entirely different route into the desert wastes roughly opposite to hers. He slung a water canteen over one shoulder, grasped the briefcase tightly, and invited Jane to join him with his outstretched free hand.

"We walk that way!" he nodded superfluously toward the barely recognizable hillock in the distance that historically signaled the position of Kilbooling Cave. He didn't waste time with self-congratulations or exclamations of 'good luck to us;' nor did Jane. In no way would either of them feel even marginally safe until they had the briefcase and the car they'd entrusted to Diane safely in Keerborg.

It wasn't long before both of the released cars almost simultaneously went ballistic. Knowing where to look, Gerald and Jane easily spotted the mushroom cloud marking each car's last moment on earth.

Though she continued to look, Jane couldn't find even a trace of whatever remained of the wreckage of Ken and Jake's previously exploded car. The same natural forces that had swept sand from the bedrock upon which they were walking, had most likely buried the wreckage. Possibly, one day (next week? next month? next year? next century?), another storm would reverse what had been covered and leave future discoverers (if there were any), wondering what the mangled, charred remains represented.

Gerald and Jane took turns carrying the briefcase.

While the going was easier than when they'd hiked the heart of the storm, it was still difficult. Solid ground existed where there had once been only sand, which made for good walking, but there was now, more often than not, two- to ten-foot sand drifts atop patches of earth that had once been easy walking but were no longer.

It was Jane who spotted the telltale red dust devil behind them whose vortex clearly indicated a car moving away from The Facility and towards them.

"It can't be a car from the car pool," Jane said. In fact, she could already tell by its beige color that it wasn't. All The Facility vehicles were white with The Facility logo emblazoned black on the driver's door.

"It does look, however, as if its point of origin was very close to The Facility," Gerald decided, based upon where the car was, where it was headed, and the dust in its wake.

"Jurgen or Sally would have probably stashed

another car somewhere, wouldn't they?" Jane's heart sank. She didn't need Gerald to answer. Of course, Jurgen would have had a car waiting somewhere in the background. He'd all but admitted to nefarious dealings like this before. All of which went to explain just why he hadn't appeared as anxious as they had imagined he would be in trying to enter the garage before Jane closed it.

Gerald computed the distance remaining to Kilbooling Cave and how long it would take Jane and him to reach it. Then, estimating the pursuing vehicle's speed, he calculated the same for it. "Maybe ... if we hurry . . ."

"Shall we bury or destroy this?" Jane lifted the briefcase which it was her turn to carry.

"Let's wait awhile and see," Gerald voted.

They headed off. Not at a faster clip, which would only have exhausted them before they could get there, but with a steady, determined pace calculated to cover the distance they needed to cover, and do it in the most expeditious manner possible.

Jane hoped the two decoy cars would afford them at least several minutes of additional time, but Jurgen didn't seem to be wasting his time following either vehicle set to fool him. Jane imagined him anticipating Gerald and her inbred intelligence and altruism that would keep them from abandoning Diane at Kilbooling Cave, and their easily apparent attraction for each other that would keep them from splitting up as the decoys were meant to suggest. Jurgen, in fact, set a direct bee-line route for the cave, and he kept to it, even though they hoped he'd not yet actually spotted the two insignificant dots that Gerald and Jane made against the storm-changed backdrop.

"I think we should dump the venom," Jane decided, "and feed the torn notebook pages to the wind." Jurgen was gaining on them fast.

Burying the briefcase was no longer a viable solution. All Jurgen would have to do was threaten to kill Gerald or Diane, and Jane would be inclined to reveal wherever the briefcase was hidden. It was all well and good to bemoan the fates of the hypothetical millions who might die up the road because of the poison and its derivatives, but Jane didn't personally know any of those likely never-to-be-seen victims. She did, on the other hand, know Diane. And she knew and loved Gerald.

Yes, she loved Gerald. She no longer harbored any doubts or reservations whatsoever about it!

She dropped to her knees in the sand, placing the briefcase carefully in front of her.

Gerald knelt down at her side. When Jane clicked open the briefcase and removed the notebook, Gerald accepted the pages she ripped from the book and gave her no argument. For him, it would be unconscionable for either of them to keep Ralph's notes or the venom as a potential means of bargaining for their lives, even if they were certain that Jurgen would live up to his side of any bargain. Unlikely, given that Jurgen had cold-bloodedly shot Sally with whom he had a far more intimate and long-lasting relationship than he'd ever had with Jane, Gerald, or Diane. And even if such an exchange were successfully made, how could Gerald or Jane live with the guilty feelings that would invariably haunt them to their dying days?!

Yes, best to get this over with, now, they both acquiesced, as Gerald ripped his pages into tiny pieces, encouraging them to blow with Jane's torn paper in the hot and heavy breeze that existed at desert ground level. Time, however, was running out so fast that he buried some of the scraps in the sand. Then, he pulled out his lighter and lit the edge of a new batch of pages. He turned the fluttering flame this way and that until it had almost completely converted the paper to ash; then, he watched the result disintegrate and blow away.

All the while, Jurgen continued his fast, relentless approach, hopefully unaware of what was happening.

"Don't get any of the poison on you!" Gerald warned when Jane fished the vial from its nest. "Gauge wind direction carefully and don't breathe even a whiff of

She hesitated, momentarily uncertain how to proceed. She'd been going to uncap the vial and merely dump the contents, but in doing so, could she be certain that none of it would touch her? Could she be sure the wind wouldn't suddenly shift just long enough for her or Gerald to inhale some of its deadly vapor? Certainly, she couldn't risk just the burial of venom, intact vial and all. No matter what the chances against Jurgen making the recovery, Jane preferred the odds absolutely against whatever scheme he might be hatching as he drove fast and furiously to reach them.

"Here," Gerald said and took the vial. He assured himself as to the direction of the existing breeze by observing where the ashes and torn shreds of paper were headed. He spotted a rock that was large enough, wasn't too close but wasn't so far as to prevent his better-than-average pitching arm from striking it with the bottle from where he was standing.

The lobbed vial exploded in a hissing cloud of

wet vapor.

Jane put the back and front covers of the notebook, still attached along their shared spine, back into the briefcase and re-snapped the metal fastening mechanisms. She kept firm possession of the case and its contents as Gerald got up and helped her to her feet. She wanted Jurgen to be continually drawn to the briefcase, like an iron filing to a magnet, no matter that the case no longer contained anything of value. As long as he spotted it when he spotted her, and he would soon spot her, if he hadn't already, he might not notice the scraps of paper blowing away in the wind, or see the smudges of disintegrated ash on the sand. Certainly, no efforts by him would be sufficient to scrounge enough venom from the millions of pieces of broken glass to reconstruct the molecular structure of the cursed poison in some all-the-money-technology-can-buy laboratory.

If they couldn't reach Kilbooling Cave by the time Jurgen overtook them, then they would still have enough time to put this spot of dumped venom and

destroyed notebook paper far behind them, even after
enfolding each other in a spontaneously sudden and eager
embrace.

Without doubt, they had just destroyed all
chances they had for a long life together. They had
burned the last proverbial bridge that might have saved
them. For the moment, they could live in peace with their
monumental decision. This was why it had been so
important that they not only make the decision, here and
now, but act on it. Later, when the reality of what they
had done sunk in—the oh-so-real end that surely awaited
them, as a result of Jurgen's inevitable wrath in having
been frustrated and then deprived of his prize—one, or
both, of them might have been tempted to save the other.
That had been the real danger. Jane would have been able
to die herself. Gerald might have done the same.
Throughout history, there had always been martyrs who
had found the fortitude needed to sacrifice for a common
cause or for a greater good. But Jane letting Gerald die,
or vice versa, all the while knowing life could be bought

for the other by merely revealing the whereabouts of one intact vial of poison and one accompanying notebook, would have been an agony of temptation not so easily overcome with a brave, *Do what you will!*

"I love you, Jane! You do know it, don't you?"

"Know it and love you equally as much."

They stole a quick kiss and another hug, then broke in mutual recognition of what they yet had to do. It would be best to be as far away from where they were now when they were caught, so there would be no hope of Jurgen attempting to salvage even one valuable scrap of information. It would also assure them of a hopefully quick demise.

Hand in hand, they turned toward Kilbooling Cave, toward a new and unexpected dust cloud that had churned to life between them and it, toward the honk of a horn from the white vehicle with a black logo on the driver's door that, like Jurgen's car, was headed in their direction.

"Diane!" Gerald defined and pointed. Both of

his arms rose above his head and waved back and forth across each other.

This car's dust plume, like that made by the opposing approach of Jurgen's car, was already fading at its point of origin, but there was no denying it came from the hillock containing Kilbooling Cave. No question, either, that it was closer to Gerald and Jane than Jurgen, and that it would reach them first with minutes to spare.

"Come on!" Gerald extended a hand, his fingers anxious to interlock with Jane's.

"I do love you!" Jane shouted into the wind. Her heart was alive with this sudden last-minute reprieve for her, for Gerald, and for their love.

They raced, all stops out, toward Diane's approaching car; Jane felt light-headed, even giddy; Gerald was wildly exhilarated. They wanted to continue to run together hand-in-hand even when they met the stopped auto whose trail of dust was overtaking the car, engulfing it and them within its protective embrace.

"Do you know how good you look?" Gerald

greeted Diane who had leaned to open the passenger door for the two of them.

"Good thing there was a pair of binoculars in the glove compartment, or I would have missed you two for sure," Diane congratulated. "I heard two explosions and figured you were goners. I was piling in to head out for Keerborg on my own when I decided to take one more look. Sally in the pursuit car?"

"Sally's dead!" Gerald informed. He'd helped Jane in with the briefcase, and he climbed in after her.

Diane was making the tight U-turn even before Gerald had the door shut. "Sally dead?"

"Have we a story to tell," Jane promised, although she hadn't nearly recovered enough second wind to attempt telling it at the moment.

Diane concentrated on maneuvering the car out of the new dust cloud it was making. "So, who's in pursuit?"

"Jurgen . . . . something or other." Jane realized she couldn't even remember the last name he'd given.

How could she have forgotten!? It would be important when the investigation began. Of course, he could have lied about this name, first and second, as easily as he'd lied about being Cole Wilcott. Then again, since he'd figured them soon to be dead . . .

"Blenge," Gerald remembered for her. "Jurgen Blenge." Although Gerald didn't, anymore than Jane, really believe the name was likely a real one.

"And however did this . . . Jurgen Blenge . . . get involved?" Diane asked, glad to be steering a course for Keerborg, rather than for a return to Kilbooling Cave.

They filled her in, since they now had the time and, finally, the breath necessary to do so. While adding back and forth to the story, Jane and Gerald kept watchful eyes on Jurgen's car, continually monitoring its progress. Diane kept a steady distance between their car and Jurgen's, feeling confident that she could continue to do so all the way to the authorities in Keerborg. She could and would, too, as long as there weren't too many unforeseen circumstances, such as . . .

"Bloody Hell, it's eaten up the roadway!" she hadn't noticed the distant storm-deposited dune though both passengers had.

"Turn to flank it," Gerald instructed.

"No going over the top?" Diane asked as she did as instructed.

"Unstable sand up top made our last attempt at crossing one of these nearly disastrous." Jane desperately wanted a car—this car—to make the trip between Kilbooling Cave and Keerborg without incident. The car, however, had already been banged up sufficiently for her to worry about it simply making the trip without falling apart.

To her surprise, as time passed, her sense of fearful excitement, even danger, ebbed with the monotony of flight. Jurgen's car remained safely at a distance. No new dunes turned up. The storm remained quiescent. Their car kept going.

The blazing heat eventually contributed to a burgeoning lethargy, as did the sameness of the landscape. Complete ennui was kept in check only by constant reminders that Gerald, Jane, and Diane were counting on constant and continued alertness to keep them alive. One mistake was all it would take to give Jurgen the advantage. From his driving, it was apparent he knew this, too.

Their jarring desert ride seemed, as Jane had wished, uneventful except for the constant bumps that were beginning to emphasize their aches and pains from simply being unable to stop and stretch.

Jane's jaws ached from her efforts to keep her teeth from clacking with each and every washboard vibration. Her neck began to ache from having to support her constantly bobbing head.

Finally, they reached the far edge of the dune, and Diane commenced the wide turn required to return to their originally interrupted bee-line to Keerborg.

Fading, first to one side and later behind them, was the steep ascent of sand they'd just skirted, as impressive as a silt-brown waterfall viewed from downriver.

Their dust trail quickly settled on the far side of the sandy hump while the rooster tail from Jurgen's vehicle continued to rise like polluted steam.

Jane knew she should have been heartened by how far Jurgen had yet to drive before he would even manage to reach the end of the dune. However, there was something about his dust plume that put her on edge.

"He's stopped!" she exclaimed loudly. While she should have been comforted by the fact, even grabbed at the assumption that his car had malfunctioned or become bogged down in sand, her mind was too busy calculating the various hypothetical alternatives that would favor Jurgen over them.

Gerald beat Jane to the punch in putting reality back into their concerns, although Jane comprehended at about the same time: "Bloody hell! He's going over the top!"

"I thought you said over the top was impossible," Diane remembered.

"For us, it was," Jane said for Gerald who had stuck his head out the window and was craning it for a better look. In point of fact, the degree of instability of any dune varied along its width, length, and height: one place unstable, a few feet away a shelf of cloaked shelf rock that could offer more than enough support for an auto to cross safely. Gerald and Jane had already been "burned" once by such an attempt and learned from their mistake. By all rights, it was Jurgen's turn. Also, there had been no immediate need for them to risk such a crossing. They had been well ahead of Jurgen. No risks taken, odds were that they would remain ahead; or, so they thought.

Risk-taking was an issue seen in an entirely different light by Jurgen, who had everything to gain and nothing really to lose by making the attempt at going over the top. It would save him minutes of valuable time that the chased trio had consumed in their circling. What's more, a successful trip over the top could possibly even put him between them and the road to Keerborg. With some fast and expert driving, Jurgen might yet intercept them before they finished their run to safety.

Jane prayed Jurgen's attempt would fail. For as hard as she prayed, she expected God at least to provide Jurgen with some difficulty. Perhaps a grain of dust would work its way into his wheels, or, for just a fraction of a second, a wheel might refuse to take hold in the sand. The sight of his car several times, each time disappearing again as sand shifted beneath its weight and slid the vehicle back down the other side of the mountain, would certainly give her hope that just possibly . . .

Jurgen's vehicle literally flew over the top, closing more distance between them so quickly they could almost make out the sickly smile on his self-satisfied face.

"No!" Jane protested. "No! No! No!"

Gerald, equally disheartened, decided to be stoic. "Jurgen has used up his luck here. We'll tap ours at Quonati Spires."

"You're kidding, right?" Diane felt hesitant to

venture.

The Spires were already visible in the distance. Nodular heaps from a distance, at closer range they resolved into pale pink mushrooms perched upon slender necks poking free of the red ground. In point of fact, each and every spire was pure white, except for a thin layer of iron-rich rock nearly at its top. This layer, however, had a tendency to bleed its color, especially during long-ago and long-forgotten rains. As a result of that bleeding, and the constant wind erosion, the white of each spire was streaked a pretty pink.

"Jurgen figures to cut us off before we make our final hook-up with the main road to Keerborg, right?" Gerald resumed. "I think we need to accept that fact and prepare for it."

"You consider Quonati Spires a viable alternative?" Diane didn't sound so sure, but she steered the car in that direction. Doing so made interception less likely than if she had kept driving toward the long-standing preferred roadway to Keerborg.

"You're not denying that the Spires offer a possible short cut?" Gerald challenged. *Possible*, though, was the operative word here, and everyone on board knew it.

While the Spires didn't look dangerous (actually, they looked benignly beautiful the closer you got to them), their eon-carved laciness was deceptive. The very delicacy of their beauty weakened each and every one of them, like a city whose buildings over the years had been invisibly tunneled by termites and were ready now to collapse at the slightest nudge. So many of the Spires had collapsed over the years, the labyrinth through them was in constant and dangerous flux. As a consequence, few people risked the inherent danger; those who did often did so to their sorrow.

"After the storm, there might not even be a pathway open," Jane reminded.

"Or, more than one new or wider pathway may have opened," Gerald was determined to be optimistic. The same winds that caused the undermining of a spire could, just as easily, sweep away fallen debris, and convert already crumbling material into passive and easily conquered sand. "The thing is," he continued, "we'll be back on a more level playing field in the Spires"

Whatever fate awaited them, there was no doubt in Jane's mind that the game that the Spires offered them was the best opportunity for temporarily reclaiming the advantage. Their change of direction had altered the angle Jurgen needed for an intercept. The three would enter the Spires before Jurgen caught up to them. After that, the deadly game they were playing would become a crapshoot with Jurgen the desperate gambler and them the house.

Of course, nothing said that Jane, Gerald, and Diane were going to be afforded a clean and easy run to the Spires. Jurgen wasn't the only adversary out there with whom they would have to contend. In fact, although Jurgen seemed of paramount importance, although the storm was seemingly over and done, Mother Nature had more at her disposal than blowing wind to make whomever forgot her sit up and take fatal notice.

It was their fast and easy approach that led Diane to believe their traverse might actually be without incident. However, a slight increase of pressure from her foot on the gas pedal, reflexively given in her anxiousness to disappear among the Spires, sent the rear-end of the car into a sudden series of heart-stopping fish-tails that sprayed unstable sand this way and that, much like a speed boat, on a zigzag course, spewed a rapidly expanding V-shaped wall of water everywhere.

The situation would have turned disastrous in the hands of a less skillful driver, but Diane had cut her teeth driving the Great Sahara. Australia's outback was simply no match for the virtual miles and miles of tiny, slippery quartz crystals that North Africa had offered up day after day.

Diane held firmly to the wheel, like a mite on a sidewinder. Not once, even for a moment, did she again ease up on the gas pedal. Her mentor, at the wheel in the Sahara, had once told her, "Attack the desert every time it attacks you, or it'll eat you alive." As a driver, Diane had no trouble viewing this desert as one giant and hungry carnivore she had to tame.

The car danced with an exuberance that turned it, more than once, through a full ninety degrees, making Jane nauseous and keeping Gerald braced against the dashboard.

Each time, when the wheels took hold, the effect was that of a bullet shot from a still-smoking gun: the g-force pushed the car's occupants back, deep into parenthesizing seats, and the vehicle jolted forward.

At Gerald's suggestion, Diane manhandled the car towards one of the dangerously narrow and shadowy areas between two particularly huge up-jutting pink-veneered columns. Applying all her attention to throwing the car full speed into a tight curve to enter the cut, she didn't notice the boulder directly in her path.

Reluctantly braking, the sliding car slipped sideways and collided with the stone in a sickening thud of deep-denting metal and bending flesh accompanied by an ear-splitting squeal of hot rubber.

Twelve

Jane was out of the car, without a memory of getting out on her own, or of anyone helping her.

The car was nearby and empty. Its motor still ran, but Jane's brief amnesia of the crash made the motor sounds seem unusual; she was unable to register the *why* of everything going on about her.

"Thank God!" Gerald appeared over her. As quickly, he was down on his knees beside her, his fingers smoothing sweat-dampened hair off her forehead.

"What happened?" She knew she was operating from within a daze.

There was no mistaking that Gerald looked worried. "The car crashed."

"Yes," Jane accepted his explanation and the memories that acceptance let flood through her. "Diane?"

"Dead."

"Ohhhhhh!" Jane shut her eyes. She was tired and sickened by so much death. Was there no end to it? Maybe if she just closed her eyes and wished …

"Jane, I need you here!" Gerald commanded her back to bleak reality. "I've got to pry back part of the front fender that's jammed against a wheel. While I'm doing that, I need you to backtrack a bit, locate Jurgen, and keep me posted as to his progress."

"How long have I been out?" Jane mechanically looked at her wrist, but her watch was gone.

"Less than a minute," Gerald assured, "but it's important we maintain whatever lead we can. At the moment, we're in a blocked corridor which means that we need to exit the Spires and try re-navigating it again somewhere else."

Scrambled senses or not, Jane knew that made them sitting ducks.

"Right!" she said; Gerald assisted her into a sitting position. She laughed at the notion that it was only fitting that a sitting duck should be sitting, but the forced humor was short-lived; it gave her a headache. Or, maybe she'd had the headache all along, the laughter just emphasizing it. Then again . . .

"Jane?"

She'd been drifting. He knew it. She knew it.

"So, I'll check on Jurgen's progress," she said and pushed herself to her feet with more than a little help from Gerald. "I'll be fine," she insisted once she felt she actually had her balance. "You tender the fender." She smiled sheepishly at her silly rhyme.

"You're sure you're fine?"

"Really, yes, I am . . . fine," she insisted and headed off, albeit so unstable on her feet that she needed to drag one hand along a crumbling rock wall to brace herself.

Once around the bend, she could see all of the way back along their narrow, empty entrance passage to where the sun came in. It looked a longer distance than she remembered having traveled, but, then, they had flown in like proverbial bats out of hell, hadn't they?

She hurried forward, counting on the dark shadows crouching around her and at the base of the Spires that would allow her silhouette to meld into the various cracks and crevices should Jurgen materialize.

At the opening that accessed the outside, light penetrated as far as the angle of the sun allowed—which wasn't far. "Where are you, Jurgen, you bastard?" she asked quietly. "You're no aborigine, like Noah, to disappear like magic."

Actually, his car proved surprisingly easy to spot in the distance, anchored as it was in the same sand trap that had caused their car to fish-tail.

"Hallelujah!" Jane shouted, not caring if Jurgen could hear her, simultaneously making sure he wasn't somewhere nearby, having abandoned his marooned car as a ploy to capture her attention while he captured her.

Jurgen, however, miraculously appeared beside his distant car and looked like he was actually out assessing damage.

Finally, a certifiable break in Jane and Gerald's favor! Jane didn't know how long it would last, but she had every intention of milking it for all it was worth.

She turned back to Gerald and reported the good news.

Their car was strongly protesting being coaxed back into movement with some unnerving metal-against-metal grating sounds, but it did move, albeit grudgingly, when and where Gerald, now behind its wheel, directed.

Jane tried to ignore Diane's body laid out to rest beneath the stones of a small stony overhang. She would have preferred taking the body along for a decent burial, but the heat, among other things, would quickly make any such humanitarianism impossible.

With no way to turn around, Gerald had to back all the way to the entrance and out onto the sun-lit red soil beyond. He was encouraged when Jurgen still appeared no closer than Jane had reported.

"Just stay stuck there until the buzzards fly in," Gerald jinxed Jurgen further.

"Amen!" Jane provided eager support.

Gerald drove the boundary of the Spires to locate another alleyway.

Reentry into the Spires meant returning into their darkness and confines: a place seemingly blacker and more claustrophobic due to the brightness of the wider-open spaces.

A Dream Time legend explained that the remains of the prehistoric deposits before them were once piled in a long-gone sea. Something about half-men-half-monsters who ticked off a snake deity and were turned to stone with the curse that they must shed their skins in perpetuity. It was a legend that seemed to presage Gerald and Jane's current situation.

Small and medium-size rocks crunched beneath the car wheels. Boulders, like the one that had blocked the first passage, could have been whittled away with a pocket knife if there had just been time. Jane and Gerald, though, couldn't linger whenever the larger masses presented themselves, so they backtracked upon every such major encounter and tried yet another route, using their amazingly still-functioning compass to keep them oriented.

The number of ways through the Spires depended upon the size and frequency of stone collapses, and whether the people aspiring to pass were on foot or driving. Sometimes, there were simply no routes through, but these two refused to accept such sentence and the fate that inevitably attended it.

Instead, they constantly pressed on, often having to go a mile the wrong way in order to gain a few yards in the right direction.

Every so often, they heard the sound of a stone, finally overburdening its support, snap like a dry twig and topple in an eventual landslide. When the sounds were close, the air became heavy and smelled of disturbed earth. There was a tale told of a prospector who died among the Spires not because he'd been buried or brained but because he'd been suffocated by the fine-grained dust.

Nor was Jane's confidence emboldened each and every time they came back upon their own car tracks. There was one hopeful aspect to it all: that their innumerable crosshatchings would confuse a pursuing Jurgen.

Gerald turned the car into a space so narrow as to allow only an inch of free space to either side. The jagged fender had already gouged a long groove into the rotten stone to one side. Could he risk going forward just because this was the first passage in ages that appeared to head a major distance in the right direction?

He stopped the car. Given the total impossibility of exiting via any door, from the inside-out, he began working to pry back the roof's damaged observation- and escape-hatch that was custom-built into all Facility vehicles. It was particularly difficult to maneuver, in that its sliding mechanism had been damaged during the car's dual rollovers back just before Noah had appeared on the scene to reveal Diane's whereabouts. Diane's hauntingly desiccated image kept appearing in Gerald's mind only to be swept away the next instant by the pressing needs of the still-living.

"Hold tight while I reconnoiter," Gerald instructed Jane when the panel finally shifted far enough for him to squeeze through onto the roof. He proceeded onto the hood, then the ground.

It was getting darker; the sun, out there somewhere, dropped deeper on the horizon. Gerald didn't look forward to spending a night here, although he couldn't imagine darkness adding much to the present seeming night of the deep channel they were currently wedged in.

His feet scrunched loose ground beneath his shoes. His mere passing caused bits and pieces to slough from weathered walls on both sides.

The passage narrowed, then suddenly expanded,

enticing with what for all purposes looked like a roadway custom-designed for them trailing off into the distance. Gerald paced the bottleneck at its narrowest point. The car should—might—make it through.

He followed the passage a few yards farther where it veered toward the right. Only a few yards beyond that, and the impasse that was the Spires ended.

Gerald didn't really believe it. Not until he stood in the opening that dumped an alluvial fan of light-colored debris, like a pink tongue, over the open red landscape. He couldn't see Keerborg, but he knew it was out there not that far away.

Rapidly lengthening shadows emphasized the scarlet, maroon, ruby, and crimson colors about him. All that red, and all Gerald could think of was the yellow chunk of cheese awaiting two famished rats at the successful completion of a laboratory maze.

He returned to the car and to Jane.

"Exit just up ahead," he reported in.

Jane hadn't expected such good news. "You're

kidding!" At the same time, she knew Gerald wouldn't be so cruel as to offer a joke at a time like this.

"There is the problem of a passageway possibly a mite too narrow for the car," he admitted. "We could leave the car and head off on foot. The walk would be long, but with a bit of luck . . ."

Jane wasn't in the mood to trust luck. If Jurgen found his own passage after they had abandoned their ride, it would seal their fate for sure. Jurgen had, after all, crossed the dune they had decided was impossible. It would be no contest as to the winner with Jurgen in a car and them on foot.

"Or, we can attempt to bulldoze our way through?" she suggested.

"Yes, there is that alternative."

"Except, one of us should be safely out of the car, just in case the sky comes falling in?"

"For which you'll want to flip a coin?"

"Heads you walk," she confirmed. "Agreed?"

"If you agree that since you flipped the coin last

time, it's my turn to flip it this time."

"Did I really flip the coin last?"

"You know you did." He flipped a coin and it came up tails.

"Two out of three?" she suggested.

"Sorry, no time."

She climbed out of the car. "How about I talk you through?"

"How about you head off to safety, and I follow only when I'm certain you're sufficiently out of the way?"

"If you insist." She moved quickly, not because she was in any hurry to see if and how he would be buried alive, but because they didn't know where Jurgen was, and time was still, proverbially, of the essence.

"Easy," Gerald talked the car into a slow crawl. "Equal distance on each side, please. No need to bring down the mountain if there's even the tiniest space to spare."

What space to spare? Gerald stopped as stone

began sloughing its pink veneer at the first bump of the vehicle's front fender against it. Bone-white sandstone fangs seemed to emerge from beneath innocuous pink.

"What now?" He backed for better realignment. Pieces of wall dumped on both fenders, but they weren't nearly as scary as the rocks that thumped nonstop off the barely reclosed hatch of the roof. "If first you don't succeed . . ."

He eased into the slot again. If the car was too big, it wasn't by more than a mere fraction, and there was always the likelihood that the walls would yield to brute persistence. Trouble was, Gerald hadn't come this far to be buried alive just feet from Jane and an exit. Then again, he was impatient to get to Keerborg, assure Jurgen's comeuppance, and enjoy some free time, out of life-threatening situations, with Jane.

"Columbus took a chance." It was, also, said that Columbus died in prison for his efforts.

The car scraped the rock pillars like a grater scraped ripe cheese, and Gerald didn't appreciate this new cheese simile at all.

Maybe if he didn't hold back, just went all out and zoomed his way through. Whatever fell, collapsed, or thundered on down, would simply fill the space he'd be vacating, and two birds would be killed with the stones: he'd be out of there, and, if their nemesis had, by chance, chosen to follow them rather than try to find a faster way around, then Jurgen would find it impossible to follow.

He gave the car more gas; his nerves were put more on edge by fingernail-on-blackboard-like screeches that hinted at more substantial stone beneath the shedding loose veneer.

Suddenly, a rock the size of a watermelon popped out of the wall onto the hood of the car and cracked open like an egg; its abandoned nest collapsing into an anthill-like dirt pile on the auto.

Gerald nearly panicked as more rocks banged helter-skelter from above. He gunned the motor, expecting more resistance, and was surprised by the fast-pace as he ripped his way through. The car skidded slightly, gouging the outside wall of the turn, and, momentarily wobbling, continued forcing its way on out into the world beyond the Spires.

Gerald braked, shouting a loud "Thank God!" that should have dislodged more boulders. He pounded the steering wheel in his excitement, then gave a start as the door on the passenger side creaked as it was yanked open.

"Can you give a girl a lift?" Jane bounded into the seat beside him; she was grinning from ear to ear.

She leaned towards Gerald, put a hand around his neck, ran her fingers through his hair, and pulled his face over close for a kiss.

"Let's go to Keerborg," he said, giving her a second quick kiss. Things looked a whole lot brighter together again: they were a formidable team.

"Maybe we should make sure our exit dislodged sufficient scree to block Jurgen should he get this far," Jane suggested.

Gerald knew a good idea when he heard one. He

opened the door and got out.

Jane joined him, and they headed back to the place they'd just exited.

They stopped at the tailings dumped during their car's departure. Now that they had escaped, they wished the trail were more impressively disrupted.

"Nothing here that Jurgen won't take at a gallop if he's half a mind," she observed. "And you and I know he is half a mind, if at all."

"Say we improve upon nature's mess?"

"With a few loud and lengthy screams?" she suggested.

"Wonderful idea," he agreed.

Their resulting shouts seemed disappointingly unimpressive, but the rocks responded otherwise.

Gerald took Jane's hand, and together the two fled the onslaught of dust and debris that tumbled from above as if waiting expectantly for the opportunity to fall when called upon.

Gerald and Jane had no sooner made their

hurried exit and shuffled to one side with their backs up flush against the outside of the last spire, than the corridor behind them coughed an explosive rush of wind, rubble and dirt.

"You okay?" Jane couldn't help her accompanying, albeit somewhat hysterical, laugh of relief.

She turned to Gerald whose shirt was open, his well-defined chest and stomach muscles sweaty and sexily revealed for Jane's viewing.

"I'm fine," he assured her.

"Yes, you certainly are that," she had to agree.

She wrapped her arms around his neck and stole some of his hard-won breath with a kiss. She felt safer than she had in a very long time. She was finally able to see the end of a very long tunnel.

"I suppose we should head on out," he suggested. Actually, he wanted another kiss, and Jane, as if reading his mind, graciously obliged.

They headed back to the car which by this time

had reappeared from the belch of dust that had temporarily engulfed everything. Gerald stopped to enjoy another kiss outside the car door when a helicopter swooped overhead and performed an aerial half-pirouette that peppered the ground, near where Gerald and Jane stood, with dust-spattering bullets.

Thirteen

Gerald's command for Jane to run for cover was superfluous, because she knew she had to run, as well as how and where: Back into the Spires—their opponents of only a short time ago were now their only hope.

Behind them, two car tires sighed, expiring from gunshot wounds that collapsed the mortally wounded car, all askew, onto two quickly flattened rubber knees.

Exhausted, Jane stumbled among the shadows and dodged a rock dislodged from somewhere above. Having gotten that far, she hypothesized, "If somehow that's Jurgen, he won't let the bullets get too close for fear of hitting what he thinks is still in the briefcase." She was breathless.

It was Jurgen, all right. His helicopter down on the ground, he cajoled them via bullhorn: "Come on, you two. Be reasonable. Give me what I want, and I'll get you safely out of here."

"Fat chance," was Gerald's opinion, "even if we had what he wanted us to give him."

"If worse comes to worst, I can let you sit out there, among those pretty pink spires, until hunger and thirst make you more reasonable," Jurgen warned.

Gerald grasped Jane's hand and led her sideways through a narrow crack in a rock wall. Jane, however, didn't feel any safer given the amount of debris they loosened on the way. She waited nervously for the landslide which thankfully never came; she was consoled, instead, by a continuing thin ribbon of twilight sky high above her.

She felt similar to when she'd foreseen the likely consequences of Gerald and her destroying the notebook and shattering the vial. This time, however, she didn't have to weigh the importance of their lives against the toxin in the wrong hands—when Jurgen discovered what they had done, their lives would be forfeit.

Gerald continued their weaving back and forth between closely located spires until they faced a solid looking wall with several ascending ledges. "Up there!" he pointed.

It was hard going. The wall, like the spires, sloughed large piles of itself beneath their weight. Gerald scrambled up to the first ledge and offered Jane a final assist by dropping to her one end of his belt and pulling. She scrambled through a waterfall of stone to join him.

She coughed and wiped her mouth.

He led her higher still, along a more gradual and less crumbly incline.

"Why be difficult?" Jurgen asked; he could hear the racket but couldn't yet locate them. "Give me what I want so we can all get on with our lives."

Gerald motioned for Jane to crawl slowly next

to him around the bend that brought them to a weather-eaten hole in what was more a ribbon of rock than a wall. The hole opened outward on the desert and afforded them an expansively revealing view while keeping them hidden in deep enough shadow for them to feel assured they couldn't be seen.

What they saw wasn't encouraging. Their car was bullet-ridden; Jurgen and another man stood beside the landed helicopter. Both Jurgen and his companion cradled menacingly large automatic weapons in their arms.

"Wouldn't you know he'd have a helicopter and friend waiting," Jane said. "The lifting weather must have allowed him to call the two into service. He must have had a radio, as well as the car, hidden all the while."

"We've plenty of food, water, and blankets, and are quite willing to share." Jurgen, the Good Samaritan, offered them sustenance: "Feel free." His laugh, though, was anything but inviting.

"Maybe I can sneak down during the night,"

Gerald conjectured.

After dark, he actually tried to do just that, over Jane's protest but failed each time because of the noise he made.

"I hear you!" Jurgen's voice would end up punctuating the gloom.

Gerald and Jane finally reconciled to settle in for the rest of the chilly night, cuddling together to keep warm. Not once did Gerald wish they hadn't gotten rid of the toxin and Ralph's notes. No way was the world safe with Ralph's research in the wrong hands. If Gerald had to die, he could think of worse ways to go than in the arms of the woman he loved.

Jane slept fitfully, trying whenever she awakened not to curse whatever fate had conspired against her long-term happiness with this man-in-a-million it had taken her so long to find. Some women never found Mr. Right, let alone shared with him all Jane had shared with Gerald.

She was asleep when the commotion began. She

awoke to a freezing morning filled with anxious thoughts that Gerald had, without letting her know, attempted, and this time been caught in, another unsuccessful assault on the enemy.

Gerald, though, was close by. He'd just moved farther out on the ledge. "There's company on the horizon!"

He pointed, but Jane had already spotted the hope-giving dot that by all rights could have been a bird but obviously wasn't.

Jurgen aimed his automatic weapon at the incoming helicopter and shot off a burst of rounds. Although even Jane knew the target was out of range, it veered off into the distance amid continuing staccato machine-gun sounds that rattled down more rocks from the Spires.

Jurgen and his companion abandoned their bedding and camp stove; the latter purposefully placed— Jane assumed— to exude early-morning breakfast smells and make the prey hungrier.

The two men scrambled into their helicopter; its rotors began whining and turning reluctantly.

"Definitely not the authorities incoming." Jane had seen many official aircraft on flyovers of The Facility, and the one fired upon didn't fit the bill.

"But obviously not friends of Jurgen, either."

"Lord be praised!" Jane said as the recently exited chopper made its reappearance.

"Attention, chopper on the ground!" said someone from the airborne craft that began to hover not far away.

Jurgen's response was more gunfire, sending the target into a long, shallow slide in the opposite direction.

"Oh, no!" Jane grabbed Gerald's arm as she conjured an image of their rescuers crashing into the ground. She was breathless when the fired-upon helicopter safely regained altitude and circled back.

It wasn't back, though, before Jurgen and his companion were fully airborne.

This time when Jurgen fired, the other copter

fired back. The aircrafts buzzed each other like dragonflies, their intricate maneuvering interrupted by seemingly stationary moments during which bullets flew fast and furiously.

"Get him!" There was no doubt for which side Jane rooted.

As if her request was all that was required, the engine of Jurgen's copter sputtered.

"Yes!" Jane exclaimed.

A hug by Gerald proclaimed his mutual excitement, agreement, and satisfaction.

Jurgen's craft went into a tilt, revolved completely around its axis, and commenced an earthward slide to completely disappear within a ground depression. Jane waited for evidence of the impact; a fireball would have been nice, but she was disappointed.

The victor didn't follow its injured prey, although Jane would have recommended it. Instead, it came in low over Jurgen's deserted camp site and settled down in a cloud of red dust of its own making.

Gerald moved nearer to the outer edge of their lair and waved both arms. Rocks dislodged at his feet, and Jane grabbed his belt from behind. The ultimate tragedy would be to lose Gerald now that rescue was impending.

A man got out and yelled something their way that neither Gerald nor Jane could understand over the noise of decelerating rotors.

Gerald cupped his hands around his mouth and yelled back. "Hello!"

Jane eyed the distant ground depression. If Jurgen's chopper resurrected, Jurgen and his companion with it, Jane wanted to be the first to know.

Gerald to Jane: "Did that guy just say he's who I think he said?"

Jane hadn't the faintest idea. She'd been too concerned that Jurgen's aircraft would rise again. "Who?"

"Would you believe, Cole Wilcott?"

"The real Cole Wilcott?" Jane did appreciate the poetic justice.

Gerald turned back to the outside and announced, "Gerald Simms and Jane Mylor!"

"From The Facility?" Cole was audible now that the rotors of his chopper had run down. "Jane Mylor, you say?"

Jane stepped forward and waved. Made uneasy by the unsteady ground, she stepped back and returned to supporting Gerald with his belt.

"Heard gunfire last night." Cole's voice sounded pure Aussie. He took off his hat and wiped his forehead. He had blond hair that showed up well in the ruddy environment. "I came to investigate but had to set down a mile from here because of engine problems. Got 'em fixed this morning and . . ." Apparently, he was tiring of their long-distance shouting conversation. "Think you could come down here?"

"You'd better watch for the guys in the other helicopter!" That was Jane's two-cents' worth. "One of them has more lives than a cat."

"There's not much chance he'll go anywhere

soon in that chopper of his, the condition I put it in," Cole predicted. "I know a mortally wounded bird when I see one."

Jane hoped so. She wanted this thing with Jurgen over and done. She was sick and tired of all the last minute, unexpected twists and turns.

Their return to the outside was easier than their climb in. If their slide wasn't so bumpy and so easily converted into a full-fledged landslide, it might have been fun — in other circumstances, it might have even made Jane feel nostalgically younger. As it was, she was simply glad to leave the Spires once and for all. The sooner she saw the last of them, except possibly from very, very far away, or in travel posters, the better she'd feel.

"Are we glad to see you!" Gerald said shaking Cole's hand vigorously.

"Ditto for me," Jane added, brushing dirt from her behind while eyeing the big man standing in front of them.

He was as tall as Gerald and possibly as muscular. He had the earned-in-the-outdoors looks of someone Jane couldn't fit behind a produce counter. In retrospect, she hadn't seen Jurgen in that role, either. Did that tell her something, or had Jurgen's charade clouded her way of seeing everything?

"I'm afraid I'm still unsure what's going on." Cole's raised eyebrow indicated a patient man whose curiosity had gotten the best of him.

"Trouble at The Facility." Jane wondered how different things would have been if she'd waited for Cole in Keerborg and not raced the storm with Gerald.

"Would you talk easier with a swallow or two of water?" Cole suggested. He produced a canteen.

"Great idea!" Gerald confirmed.

Jane could only agree, although this water, like all the rest she had tasted throughout Australia, was never the same as what she savored at home.

"Now, since I seem to have spoiled breakfast plans here," Cole said, back in possession of the canteen and motioning toward the blackened pan of burned-to-point-of-disintegration food still on the stove, "what do you say to my flying you to someplace a bit more congenial?"

Maybe it was because Jane had been fooled one too many times not to be wary now, but she felt a paranoia that wouldn't go away. "Cole, did you happen to bring any jicama?"

Gerald was confused: that was expected. Cole was confused: that wasn't expected — or was it?

Jane's insides went icy.

"Maybe an avocat concombre?" she suggested.

Cole and Gerald looked at each other and then eyed her curiously.

"A what and what?" Cole asked, vocalizing Gerald's thoughts exactly.

"Oh, I forgot," Jane dismissed as breezily as her rapid heartbeat would let her, "you don't know what those are, do you, Cole?" She waited to hear him say it.

Gerald could have given her a rough translation

of the French, for the latter at least, but what did an avocado-cucumber have to do with anything? "I'm afraid I don't know what you're talking about, either," he voiced in disbelief.

Jane wouldn't have known either of the vegetables, until three years before, when she'd visited a London greengrocer looking for something exotic for a special dinner. Granted, it hadn't been a store that was part of the then extensive Wilcott chain, but . . . "You know to what I'm referring, Cole?"

"I'm afraid I really don't."

Jane kicked him in the shin. When he reflexively shifted his weight to his other leg, she kicked that shin, too, and gave him a shove she frustratingly realized wasn't enough to topple him—until it did.

"Another imposter!" Jane counted on Gerald to come to her assistance, no questions asked.

Unfortunately, Gerald was too slow, or, more likely, their adversary was too quick. The man arched his back and sprang back to his feet, throwing Gerald a direct punch to the chin. Then, he whirled on Jane.

Jane, however, was ready for him and kicked him mercilessly "where the sun don't shine."

His response was a loud grunt, an equally loud exhalation of breath, and a doubling over that proved long enough for Gerald to recover and down him with two thudding judo chops, one to the solar plexus, followed by another across the back of the neck.

Gerald and Jane undid the man's belt and shoe laces to tie him up. Only then did Gerald ask: "Jicama? Avocat concombre?"

"Exotic vegetables, once merely a fad, now staples in many major supermarkets. Cole, still in the grocery business when the craze began, was one of the first to jump on the bandwagon. Or, so Mrs. Cooper told me over a jicama and avocat-concombre salad."

"But what made you suspicious enough of this guy even to ask?"

"Rampant paranoia?" Jane suggested. "One imposter, why not two? Woman's intuition? Sixth sense?

His accent too Aussie? And I couldn't picture him selling groceries."

"Smart lady! Now, if this were other than real life, I would whisk you to that helicopter and fly you out of here. However, I don't know the first thing about flying a helicopter, do you?"

"I wish I did."

"Don't completely despair! I should at least be able to figure out its radio. Clear skies—" Gerald checked the horizon over Keerborg as if he expected a storm to suddenly materialize out of nowhere; Jane caught herself checking, too: nothing would surprise her. "—tell me we just might be successful in summoning someone."

Gerald didn't need Jane to tell him his idea was a good one, and he didn't waste the time asking. Jane stayed put to make sure their belt- and shoestring-tied captive didn't perform any Houdini prestidigitations.

Seconds later, Jane regretted she'd stayed behind, because Jurgen's helicopter suddenly rose from the ground depression, like a Phoenix from its ashes;

Gerald's SOS had apparently reached the wrong ears. Not that Jane was surprised; the dogfight between Jurgen and his stooge, Jane now knew, had been staged entirely for Gerald and Jane's benefit.

If before, Jurgen hadn't let the bullets get too close, because he could see Jane with both Gerald and the briefcase, Gerald was now expendable.

Jane, briefcase in hand, screamed, "Gerald!" and raced towards the grounded helicopter, from which Gerald's feet protruded. Jurgen, though, flew faster and began riddling the whole of the downed aircraft with an unrelenting barrage of gunfire that started as thumping dust-eruptions and progressed to dull pings until the bullets had riddled the metal like Swiss-cheese.

Dare to Love in Oz

Fourteen

"Gerald!" Jane reached the bullet-ravaged helicopter before Jurgen could maneuver for a second round. She was horrified to find Gerald wounded, one hand limply holding onto the microphone of a radio made inoperative by the strafing.

Still conscious, Gerald's immediate concern wasn't for his condition but for Jane's safety. "Run, Jane!"

Even if Jane were willing to leave him, which she was not, she would have been blocked by Jurgen's chopper setting down, close by, between her and the

Spires.

Gerald's attempted smile would have been more reassuring if it weren't so distorted from pain. "Remind me, when we're out of this, to take flying lessons to cover future contingencies," he bantered breathlessly.

Jane appreciated his humor but couldn't muster any on her own. The blasted chopper interior, plus the sudden smell of gas, told her they were lucky to be alive. "Where are you hit?"

"Hard to tell." Gerald grunted; the shock and trauma that had momentary served as a partial analgesic hadn't yet worn off. "Ask me again when . . ." Gerald went silent.

Jane yanked the helicopter's first-aid kit free of its restraining clamps. Jurgen, though, gun in hand, wasn't disposed to her playing Florence Nightingale. "Out!"

She turned on him with vehement fury. "He's bleeding!"

"I shot him, remember?" Not an iota of

compassion. "Now, out! Both of you."

Jurgen's helping hand on Jane's arm felt like a vise, and she was pulled out; she just had time to bring the briefcase with her. The extraction of Gerald was less humanitarian; Gerald groaned when tossed onto the sand.

"Brute!" Jane accused. She went to Gerald and bent down to diagnose his wounds.

Jurgen didn't seem in the least phased by Jane's low opinion of him. "I believe you have something of mine. So, if you'll please hand it over, we can get over with this."

"This," Jane said and elevated the briefcase for his look-see, "isn't going to do you any good." For the first time, she wished the poison and the notebook were still intact so she could at least try using them as a bargaining chip to save Gerald. That and buy them more time.

"Just hand it over, Jane. Admittedly, you gave me a good run for my money, but the odds were always in my favor."

Jane handed it over, but she was determined to keep him from shooting the both of them until he learned the truth. "You might want to check inside."

Jurgen backed away from her for a few feet and knelt in the sand; his gun still pointed towards Gerald and Jane as he disengaged the case's latches with his other hand, and the lid flipped opened.

"I see." Jurgen didn't sound nearly as surprised as Jane expected.

So, why wasn't he ranting and raving? Why a mere, "Hid the poison and Ralph's notebook somewhere, did we?"

"Destroyed them, you bastard!" Gerald managed; Jane would have drawn out the revelation, playing for time, but maybe Gerald was right in not prolonging the inevitable.

"Let's just step back a moment," Jurgen suggested, "and let me tell you just why it's so important that neither of you waste my time, or yours, with more game-playing. To speed things along: remember the kind offer of water made to you by my associate when he finally coaxed you out of hiding? If my memory serves me correctly, you didn't take any water into the Spires with you, during your foot race to hide. You surely emerged this morning rather thirsty, yes? Enough so as to have indulged his offer?" His leer was as disconcerting as his chuckle was malevolent. "So, you've drunk enough muir-snake toxin to kill you several times over."

"You're bluffing!" Gerald didn't sound convinced.

"Oh, but I kid you not!" Jurgen sounded self-satisfied enough to make the likelihood feasible. "Cross my heart."

Jane began a mental rundown of her body functions and how they would be altered if what Jurgen said was true. Her heartbeat was rapid, but that could be attributed to events, rather than to toxin. Likewise, her sweat was a logical response to the circumstances.

"I decided it a good back-up option to get from you what I wanted should you have hidden it somewhere along the long and dusty way." Jurgen looked directly at Jane.

Jane suddenly didn't feel at all well.

"Oh, yes!" Jurgen reached into his pocket and produced an ampoule. "And I was considerate enough to bring along the antidote."

The way he held it out, so invitingly, told Jane he was waiting for her to make a grab. She didn't, and she was rewarded with his okay-don't-amuse-me smirk.

"My proposition is pure and simple," he informed. "You take me to what I want, and I give you both what you want, actually need, for your continued survivals."

"What guarantee do we have that you'll live up to your side of the bargain?" Jane didn't like Gerald's continued grimaces of pain and wished she were free to attend to him. His being yanked from the helicopter had caused his wounds to begin bleeding profusely.

"My word is my bond!" Jurgen looked and sounded insulted that she considered anything more was

William Maltese

needed.

Jane and ashen-faced Gerald laughed in unison at Jurgen's play-acting. Whether serious in his offer, or not, Jurgen seemed anything but amused.

"Nonetheless, my word is all you'll have, so we might as well move on from there," he decided for the three of them, "before it's simply too late."

"And if we don't have the toxin you want, or the notebook to go with it?" Jane, like Gerald before, saw little point in further stalling. If Gerald and she had truly drunk muir-snake toxin, and Jurgen was definitely Machiavellian enough to have had the offered water doctored by his smarmy cohort, knowing Gerald and Jane would emerge from the Spires thirsty, the faster things moved the better. The wicked queen in Snow White couldn't have been more skillful than Jurgen in getting victims poisoned.

"You've seen the empty briefcase," Gerald said. "We gave the contents a toss."

"Of course you did," Jurgen's tone remained

calm and disbelieving, "and as soon as you tell me where, this nastiness can be over."

So new nastiness can begin? "I don't know where," Jane said. Probably true, in that she'd made it a specific point not to register any reference points or landmarks in her mind.

"There was always the possibility that you'd win, and this interrogation take place," Gerald said. "We didn't want to face the moral dilemma of handing something so deadly over to you in order to save ourselves."

"Is this some kind of comedy routine?" Jurgen didn't sound amused. "If so, you two really must take it on the road."

"We're not joking." Jane was delighted and saddened by her admission.

"Maybe I won't wait for the poison to work." Jurgen moved the barrel of his gun back and forth between Gerald and Jane in emphasis. "Maybe I'll show you that I mean business by putting a bullet in—" He

paused and shifted the gun barrel towards Gerald. "—
Gerald's skull, right here and now." A puff of breeze
wafted the smell of metal and gun oil in Jane's direction.

"No!" she protested.

"I know the two of you have something
romantically going on between you; I could tell as much
at first glance. Aside, I mean, from your present plot to
keep from me what I want. So, are we talking true love
here, or what?"

Jane's feelings were none of his business. What
did he know of love anyway? Jane doubted even his
mother could love such a monster.

"Well, I'm counting that the last thing a woman
in love wants to see is her one true love's brains blown
out," Jurgen confided.

"If what you want was salvageable, I'd tell
you." Suddenly, Jane wasn't lying, either.

Jurgen pulled back the hammer on his revolver
and walked over to put the gun barrel to Gerald's head.
"If you love him, you'll save him."

"I do love you, Gerald. I do!"

"I know, Jane. Believe me, I do know."

"So, all that stands between you two and a happy-ever-after ending is a tiny bit of information to be passed on to me," Jurgen concluded.

"Maybe we could take you there." Who was Jane trying to kid? Without specific reference points, they could wander the area for years and never find the exact place.

"Maybe?" Jurgen wasn't thrilled by her insinuated uncertainty. He pulled the gun away from Gerald and aimed it at her. "What do you take me for, a fool? Do you honestly believe that I believe that you chucked a prize whose value you knew full well when you ran off with it?" His arched eyebrow signaled a bulb suddenly lighting in his brain. "Or is it because it is so valuable that you ran off with it in the first place?"

"No!" Jane knew where this was going, and he was dead wrong.

"What you really want is money, yes?" Jurgen

came very close to making that a statement. "Who gives a tinker's damn about anything but big dollars? Is that how this routine goes?"

"No!"

Jurgen ignored Jane's continued denial. "Well, name your price, and we'll bargain from there. Just remember that I hold certain key cards in this poker game. Your life is worth a large deduction from the going price. Gerald's life should warrant another."

"I don't want your filthy money!" she insisted. "I want you out of our lives. I'd tell you what you want to know, if I only knew it."

"My patience is unfortunately nearing its end." Jurgen put the gun back to Gerald's head. "Your bluff has been brilliant, in its own way, but a good player knows when to lay down her hand and quit. Whatever you feel for Gerald, Jane, may, in the end, have to be shared with him in heaven—if you really think that's where the two of you are headed for holding out on me like this."

Jurgen's finger tightened on the trigger.

"Please, don't kill him." Jane wanted to scratch out Jurgen's eyes, and she would have if she could have before he could shoot Gerald.

"Enough, now!" Jurgen insisted. "More than enough! I'm going to count to five." His gun was still aimed at Gerald's head. "We all know from the movies what happens when at five."

"You might as well save your breath and pull the trigger now." Gerald was dealing with a huge combination of physical and mental pain that had begun rising to the surface over the last few minutes: the blessed numbness of original shock and trauma was long gone and all that was left was raw pain and agony. "Neither of us can resurrect the smashed vial, or the notes we burned, no matter what you offer or threaten."

"One . . . two . . . three . . ." Jurgen paused when Jane covered her eyes. "Open your eyes, Jane!" he commanded. "I want you to remember the last look in your lover's eyes as he meets his doom all because of you."

She refused. If he did what he said he was about to do, she couldn't watch. It was already too much to bear the guilt of knowing she could have extracted Gerald from this horror if she'd only held back, and . . .

"Jane, Jane, Jane." Jurgen was conciliatory, as if his outburst had surprised even him, and he was out to make amends. "Shall I list the various ways that have been used, since before Genghis Khan, to make someone see something he or she doesn't want to see? The easiest way involves a knife and the eyelids. I have a knife. You have the eyelids."

Jane opened her eyes.

"Four . . ." Jurgen resumed his count.

"It's all right, Jane." Gerald didn't want his death to be this painful for her. If he weren't so drained of strength . . .

"Five!" said Jurgen and pulled the trigger.

The gun hammer clicked against an empty chamber and made Jane's heart stop. Her legs went rubbery, and she couldn't stand up. Accompanying her collapse was a flood of tears . . . from hurt, frustration, helplessness, hate . . . and from the pure joy of realizing that Gerald was still alive.

Jurgen hissed a menacing and bone-chilling sound. Jane assumed it was due to his anger at his gun having malfunctioned. She was wrong.

"I now believe you!" His accusation was without forgiveness. "You stupid, do-gooder fools!"

Jane experienced a surge of hope but knew she was Pollyanna to expect mercy for having finally convinced him.

Her mind flashed a lexicon of potential horrors. Gerald, too, was entertaining visions of what the thwarted Jurgen might now try to do. A surge of adrenaline propelled him forward. He was genuinely surprised when Jurgen moved so fast. Jurgen's gun thumped against the back of Gerald's passing neck.

Gerald's fall was long and hard. It finished with what seemed to him a submersion beneath a tidal wave of agony that crashed onto him and then washed him from every direction, threatening him with drowning in complete darkness. Only his hope that he might yet be able to do one last thing for Jane thrust him back through the excruciating fog.

He opened his eyes just in time to see Jane downed by a backhand from Jurgen and her tormentor bend down over her semiconscious body. Gerald tried to get to his feet, but his bad leg buckled. "Leave her alone I said . . ."

"I heard you the first time." Jurgen stood and turned, displaying an empty syringe in his hand. "You're misplaced concern is over nothing. In fact, I've merely given your girlfriend the antidote that's going to save her miserable life."

Gerald was confused. He shook his head to clear it. Jane was obviously conscious, if still dazed.

"Now, for you." Jurgen held up the antidote and filled the barrel of the syringe with it. Without moving, he squirted the contents of the syringe into the air. "Ooooops!"

"Why?" Jane was horror-struck. There was something totally perverse at work here. She wasn't sure she wanted to hear what it was, but she was sure Jurgen would tell her.

"'Why?' you have the audacity to ask?" Jurgen said and whirled on her, "You bloody jillaroo!" His face was beet red, and Jane suspected that his coloring had nothing to do with the rapidly increasing morning heat. She was right. "You've inconvenienced me, and we're talking major inconvenience, here. That's why. I want your punishment to fit the extent of your meddling. So —" Jurgen filled the syringe again, this time completely draining the containing ampoule. He squirted the retrieved liquid onto the warm sand. "—I want you, Jane, alive for a very long time, in order for you to know that what happened here was because you went against me and thought, for however short awhile, that you were the clever winner. As soon as I'm out of here and enough time has elapsed so I'm quite certain Gerald is dead of the poison, I'll personally call the Keerborg authorities to see that you're rescued. Don't think you giving them the name Jurgen Blenge is going to do you or them any good; I assure you, it's no more my real name than Cole Wilcott ever was."

"You won't get away with this." Jane was embarrassed by the dying weakness of her threat.

Jurgen capped the needle with its protective plastic guard and slipped it back into his pocket. "Here!" He tossed her the empty ampoule. "A souvenir for you."

Reflexively, Jane caught the small bottle. Its empty interior sparkled briefly in the glaring sunlight. Tears sparkled with equal intensity in her eyes.

"After Gerald passes into the great beyond, and before your rescue arrives, feel free to play Hamlet and contemplate that empty vial, instead of Yorick's skull," Jurgen invited.

Jane was down and crying helplessly as Jurgen untied his henchman; the two men boarded the functional helicopter, kept at ready by the pilot on board, and lifted off. The total horror of Jane's situation suddenly erupted inside her, and, struggling to her feet, she raised her arms and screamed, "Kill me, too!" How could she go on with Gerald soon to be dead? "Come back and finish it!"

They didn't come back. Instead, they evaporated into the painfully blue Australian sky.

"Jane?" How many times did Gerald have to say it to get her attention? Five? Ten? Fifteen? However many, it was important he penetrate her obvious distress.

"I can't!" she moaned, and that summed it up: can't cope; can't live; can't die; can't stop crying. "I can't go on knowing I've lost you this way."

"You can and will." Gerald refused to die before he salvaged her sanity. "You tell me why."

Was Gerald mad! Jane knew, but couldn't say it to him.

So, Gerald told her. "Because I'm glad that my dying will at least save you. Do you hear me, Jane? I'm glad! It gives my death meaning."

She cradled his head in her lap and smoothed his hair off his burning forehead. She told herself again and again he wasn't going to die; he, though, knew it was important she didn't indulge that illusion.

"I'm going to die, Jane." He took her hand and squeezed so hard the pain forced her to focus on what he said. "Me dead, but how many lives have been saved, yours included? How many perfect-crime assassinations thwarted? How many lifelines preserved because the stuff wasn't brewed in a giant vat and sprayed on the inhabitants of some country who disagreed with some other country's politics? You have to get out of the purely personal tragedy rut and see the bigger picture that resulted when we disposed of the toxin and the notebook."

"I thought it would be both of us dead, if the time came." Jane wiped away the tears that had splattered Gerald's face and left asterisks of clean skin upon his otherwise dusty features. "I never thought it would just be you."

"Do you think you're doing me justice by assuming I'm any less altruistic than you? You're not a female chauvinist pig, are you?"

"No." She leaned and kissed his damp forehead.

He controlled his tears, not because he thought it unmanly to cry, but because he didn't want her to think he said one thing and felt another. He wanted to go out heroically; few people had that opportunity. It was important to him that he die with dignity, given the chance. It was important a dying man leave the woman he loved with a reason to go on living without him. "Someone once told me the ancient Egyptians thought a person wasn't really dead as long as he was remembered."

"Wrong country," she observed wryly.

"Just promise me that you'll remember me on occasion. Not enough to interfere with someday marrying someone else and ..."

"I'll never marry someone else!" she interrupted.

"If I believed that, it would make me very sad, indeed, because I know how very much you have to offer,

Jane. I'd hate to think of all that shut up inside of you just because I had to die here and now."

She put her fingers to his lips and silenced him. She knew he was trying to prepare her for survival, and she fully knew she would eventually have to deal with a future without him, but she didn't want to hear of it now.

She made a concentrated effort to deal with the present predicament. It would do Gerald, holding up so well, no good to witness her disintegration. Later, if she had to, she'd indulge herself and really fall to pieces.

"I've a few things to do." Muir-snake poisoning, particularly nasty in its final stages, never finished off anyone in minutes. The process was long and drawn-out; Jane resolved to make Gerald as comfortable as possible.

She retrieved a first-aid kit from the bullet-ridden car, and another from the bullet-ridden helicopter; she doctored the two bullet wounds, one in his left leg, and the other in his left shoulder. She rejected the available morphine, fearing it might kill him in his weakened condition; instead, she gave him several pain pills washed down with water scrounged from the leftovers of Jurgen's camp. No way, she figured, would such water be poisoned if Jurgen intended for her to survive this ordeal.

It was growing viciously hot, but it wasn't likely Gerald could make the shade of the Spires without a prolonged, painful, and likely fatal shuffle. Even if Jane could somehow get him there, they would have had to maintain a constant vigil for falling rocks. Instead, she constructed a lean-to from the tarp that came with the car survival gear. The canvas had a few bullet holes, but none so large that they admitted much sunshine.

She stockpiled supplies and took a sight inventory. Jurgen had left plenty for them until his delayed phone call summoned someone eventually to get her.

Jane fixed Gerald and herself something to eat. Muir-snake poison eventually would affect his larynx, and he wouldn't be able to swallow or, later, breathe. To prepare for the latter, Jane laid aside antiseptic, some tubing, and a knife for whenever the tracheotomy might be necessary.

She put the garbage in a bag. Gerald loathed littering, and Jane had no intentions of insulting his sensibilities at this time in his life. "Anything else I can get you?" She avoided any similarity to a guard asking a condemned man his last request.

"Actually, I don't feel half bad." In truth, he didn't feel half good, but he had always been a man who could look at a partial glass of water and optimistically see it as half full. "How about you just hold my hand?"

First, Jane soaked a rag with water and wiped his sweaty brow; then, she held his hand. His sweating would get worse as the poison spread.

"Nice." If he could preserve the moment forever, he could have lived with it. The pills were countering just enough pain to make it tolerable. The toxin hadn't yet taken such a hold that it screwed up his nervous system the way he knew it soon would.

"I just wish there were something more I could

do." Then, it struck Jane that there *was* something. Why go to defeat without every option explored? "Don't go away, will you?" she said with an attempt at levity in her voice, so Gerald wouldn't think her as deeply in the dumps as she was.

He appreciated her effort. "I was just about to run the mile."

"It'll have to wait." She patted his hand and laid it with his other on his chest.

First off, she had to be sure about the condition of the car. She headed over to it, got in behind its steering wheel, turned the key still in its ignition; she wasn't surprised when she heard no noise whatsoever from the damaged engine.

Leaving the car, she walked to the derelict helicopter. Once again, she smelled fuel leaking from the aircraft.

"Jane!" Gerald was propped on his elbows. He'd seen her on the move, and he intuitively sensed what she was now thinking. "Use the propane canister from Jurgen's camp stove as a starter. Open it up, stuff in a rag, light the rag, and throw it at the copter."

Jane headed for the camp stove and followed Gerald's directions to the letter.

The copter fuel ignited with a *POOF* not nearly as loud as Jane expected.

The heat of the explosion, however, hit her full-force. The immediate smell of singed hair had her quickly checking to make sure she wasn't also on fire.

Gerald saw and gave an appreciative yell that was less loud than he wanted; partial paralysis had already begun to set into his throat.

Jane was disappointed, in that the fire was almost smokeless and so transparent she could see the desert landscape on its other side.

"Jack up the car, and add the four wheels to the fire," Gerald encouraged hoarsely.

Jane did just that, all the while knowing this, like everything else she now did, was consuming precious minutes. If it was all for naught, she would always regret that she hadn't spent the time at Gerald's side. Her only consolation, once she had done all she figured she could do, was that Gerald obviously hadn't begrudged her efforts or any of the time she'd been gone from him.

"Job well done!" he congratulated in a raspy growl when she finally resumed her rightful place beside him and returned his hand to hers.

Epilogue

Gerald was sitting up in bed when Jane came into the hospital room and kissed him hello.

"You just missed Cole and Riala." His voice was hoarse, his neck bandaged where the tracheotomy tube had only recently been removed.

"Actually, I caught them on their way out." Jane pulled a nearby chair closer to the bed and sat in it. "It provided us with one more opportunity to marvel at the irony of the real Cole, after so many fakes appearing, actually flying in to our rescue."

"I particularly enjoy the part that had Cole

getting to Keerborg and finding Riala, instead of you; Riala so worried she had bundled you off too hastily into a deadly storm, communications to The Facility down even after the storm had blown over, that she insisted Cole fly her to The Facility to be sure you made it there safely."

"Catching only part of the brief SOS you managed to get out." Jane was delighted to enjoy, marvel, and re-live right along with him. "Not enough of it, though, for them to pinpoint our location."

"That last bit of homing-in accomplished by—tah-dah—your cleverness in setting the derelict copter afire," he added.

"And by—tah-dah—your cleverness in insisting I add the car tires to the blaze to blacken its smoke," she completed. "Now, after all this mutual backslapping, are you ready for some additional good news?"

"Better news than Cole and Riala seriously dating, you mean? I still worry, you know, now that Cole's seen what a prize you are in person."

Jane laughed. "Cole could want me all he wants, but he could never have me. I've gone through too much to let myself slip away from you at this hard-won juncture."

"You do know how to make this man happy."

"How about I make you even happier by telling you the police have picked up Jurgen, or whatever his name really is?"

"Tell me you're not kidding!"

"I'm not kidding. His mistake was in keeping to his word to call the authorities when he figured you were dead and gone. Of course, we have Cole to thank for his police connections that kept our rescue under wraps as far as Jurgen was concerned."

"They traced the bastard's incoming call?"

"As far as Sydney. Always the clever one, Jurgen didn't stay on the phone long enough for a complete trace."

"So, if the police couldn't trace his call?"

"He was at the Sydney airport, headed for Hong

Kong, nabbed courtesy of my efforts and those of a police sketch artist. The likeness was immediately faxed round and about, including to Sydney. He was apprehended with three different passports, by the way. No one yet knows his real name, and he hasn't been all that cooperative. His associate, the second pseudo Cole Wilcott of our adventure, was picked up along with him. The police are delighted to have the two and figure they can play one against the other until one cracks; not that either is apt to reveal much of genuine worth. Still . . ."

"So, when do I get out of here so we can celebrate in style?" That was what Gerald wanted to know. "I've an engagement ring to buy and a proposal to make."

"That's your way of asking me to marry you, is it?"

"Maybe if I knew you would say yes, I could be more direct."

"You do know that, after all we've been through, we should probably spend a little time getting our thoughts and emotions together."

"I've already spent all the time I need here in this hospital bed doing just that."

"Okay, then, ask me the question, and I'll say yes."

"Will you marry me?"

"Yes."

She reached for his offered hand and gave its callused palm an oh-so gentle and loving kiss.

Dare to Love in Oz

About the Author

William Maltese was born in the Pacific Northwest. He has a B.A. in Marketing/Advertising and spent an honorable tour of duty in the U.S. Army, achieving the rank of E-5. He started his authorial career, which has now extended over four decades, by writing for men's pulp magazines. He has penned more than 200 books, both fiction and nonfiction. His esteemed credentials have earned him, among many other accolades, a listing in the prestigious WHO'S WHO IN AMERICA. His websites include:

http://www.williammaltese.com
http://www.myspace.com/williammaltese
http://www.myspace.com/draqual
http://www.myspace.com/flickerwarriors
http://www.myspace.com/maltesecandlegallery
http://www.mxi.myvoffice.com/williammaltese

Dare to Love in Oz

If you enjoyed *Dare to Love in Oz* consider
these other fine Books from
Savant Books and Publications:

Aloha from Coffee Island by Walter Miyanari
Essay, Essay, Essay by Yasuo Kobachi
A Whale's Tale by Daniel S. Janik
Tropic of California by R. Page Kaufman
The Village Curtain by Tony Tame

Scheduled for Release in 2009:
Today I am a Man by Larry Rodness
The Bahrain Conspiracy by Bentley Gates
The Mythical Voyage by Robin Ymer
The Jumper Chronicles: The Quest for Merlin's Map
by W. C. Peever

If you are an author or prospective author who would like
to be published
contact Savant Books and Publications at
http://www.savantbooksandpublications.com